The
Library of
Heartbeats

Laura Imai Messina was born in Rome and moved to Tokyo at the age of 23. Her international bestselling novel *The Phone Box at the Edge of the World* was published in 31 countries. Laura teaches at some of the most prestigious Japanese universities, as well as writing for newspapers and working with the Japanese National TV Channel NHK.

Lucy Rand was shortlisted for the TA First Translation Prize for *The Phone Box at the Edge of the World* which she translated while living in Japan. She has also translated novels by Italian authors Paolo Milone and Irene Graziosi, and is the editor of the guided audiobook app, Audrey. She now lives in Norwich.

The
Library of
Heartbeats

**To find what you have lost
You must listen to your heart**

Laura Imai Messina

Translated from the Italian by Lucy Rand

**MANILLA
PRESS**

First published in Italian as L'ISOLA DEI BATTITI DEL CUORE
in 2022 by Piemme
Published in agreement with MalaTesta Lit. Ag., Milano
First published in the UK in 2024 by
MANILLA PRESS
An imprint of Zaffre Publishing Group
A Bonnier Books UK Company
4th Floor, Victoria House, Bloomsbury Square, London, WC1B 4DA
Owned by Bonnier Books
Sveavägen 56, Stockholm, Sweden

A CIP catalogue record for this book is available from the British Library.

Hardback ISBN: 978-1-78658-311-6
Trade paperback ISBN: 978-1-78658-312-3

Also available as an ebook and an audiobook

5 7 9 10 8 6 4
Typeset by IDSUK (Data Connection) Ltd
Printed and bound in Great Britain by Clays Ltd, Elcograf S.p.A.

Manilla Press is an imprint of Zaffre Publishing Group
A Bonnier Books UK company
www.bonnierbooks.co.uk

To Francesca, who changed my life
and to the one billion, four hundred
million heartbeats that have brought
me this far.

A note on the language

The Hepburn Romanisation system has been used for the transcription of Japanese terms, according to which, vowels are read as short vowels in English (like the *a* in *cat*, *e* in *edge*, *i* in *igloo*, *o* in *octopus* and *u* in *umbrella*) unless they carry a macron (ō), which doubles the length of the vowel sound. The *g* sound is hard, like in *pig*, *f* is pronounced more like *h*, and *r* something more akin to *l*.

Following the Japanese convention, surnames precede first names.

In the south-west of Japan, in a puddle of sea shared by two prefectures called Kagawa and Okayama, floats a little island that is like nowhere else on earth: Teshima.

Starting in the capital, you take a plane, then a boat, then a bus, and a lot of steps to join them up.

On the eastern tip of the island, sheltered from view, sits a small building with a huge window looking out over the sea. Inside is a catalogue of the heartbeats of tens of thousands of people from all over the world, some who are still with us, others already shadows.

It is called Shinzō-on no Ākaibu, the **Heartbeat Archive**.

Part One

ばくばく *baku baku*

Lies mend life and make it more beautiful, and since no one knows what the truth is, it isn't very important.

—Christian Boltanski

Teshima, Autumn

豊島 秋

'DO YOU HEAR IT?' ASKS the boy, turning to the man.

At the exact time of the question, the man is forty years old and the valves of his heart have opened and closed around one billion, four hundred and seventy million times. Since three hundred and thirty-three days ago, he has started to call things by their names again; he has started being concerned with where the world is heading again – who will win the elections in Japan, how long it will take mankind to fill the sea with plastic. And, once again, he is afraid of dying.

'Do you hear it?' the child repeats. His question is like a prayer, because if an adult hears it too, it means it's real.

'Not yet.'

It is only after they have left the trail that slips between little houses built from wood and metal sheets, when the landscape of Teshima splits in two, and green paddy fields unfold around them, that the air starts to vibrate more powerfully.

The child does not repeat his question but observes the man intently.

The man nods this time. Now he can feel it.

To contain his emotion, he crouches down to the height of the small human in front of him, still like Moses in the act of parting the waters.

If before they could hear nothing, now there is nothing but sound. *Pam pam, bam bam, doki doki, thump thump.* The hill is pulsing.

The boy places his hand over his chest and closes his eyes.

Doef doef, boum boum, tu tump.

'We must be close.'

This island is a heart. It contracts with the irregular beat of the waves. The tides prolong its pulse, a beat or two is sometimes skipped. But it always begins again.

In the months leading up to this day, the boy and the man have been learning about how the sounds that are most pleasant to human beings – a certain piece of music, a montage in a film, the waves lapping the shore – resonate with the internal patterns of our minds. It is called *1/f fluctuation* and it is the same pattern that is observed in a heartbeat. It is something that seems continuous but is in fact continuously changing.

The child gets down on all fours and presses his ear against the ground between the rice fields.

The man doesn't stop him; he suddenly remembers when he was six and lay down in the road to get an ant's eye view of the world. The sensation of leaving no trace. Everything should start, he thought, with observing things from where they are. His mother, next to him, hadn't stopped him either. 'We have to understand as many creatures as we can, even the ones that are most different from us, if we want to understand ourselves,' she always said and he, to test the truth of that statement, justified every bizarre thing he did by saying he was trying to understand.

The man now remembers how, right there in the middle of the city, he had experienced vertigo for the first time, a reminder of the planet's incessant rotation, despite seeming to stand still.

The boy is experiencing the same sensation, only he is feeling the air pulsate.

The boy gets back up. 'I'm hungry. Can we eat?'

'Yes, of course.' The man pulls two *onigiri* from his rucksack. They sit down on the edge of a rice field.

After a number of beats in the air, the rhythm pauses. A long moment of silence follows, and then it starts again.

A handover: one heart letting another speak.

It's October. The fields are chirping with all the summer that, in two days of unexpected autumnal warmth, seems to have returned to Teshima. It has duped the dragonflies that have taken flight again, and the cicadas which, having burrowed underground, have re-emerged in full song.

Every so often, the boy kneels down and pokes his finger into the cicadas' holes.

'We're really close. The map says it's just a few hundred metres as the crow flies.'

'Is it over there?' the boy points.

'Yes, let's go.'

The man still doesn't know what they'll find on the other side of the hill. He has his suspicions but knows nothing for certain. Like how we know nothing of time while we are living it.

The boy doesn't know anything either, but he's used to not knowing. To make up for it, he falls in love more easily – with this unexpected trip, with the man's care for him, with the idea that the sound of people's heartbeats has a place in the world – and this makes him happy.

They climb up the slope that leads to the Karato Hachiman shrine, then turn right as the map indicates, pushing branches out of the way with their arms. The sea is on their left.

The sound of the heartbeats gets louder as, hand in hand, they approach the small building.

They both tread cautiously, as if over a minefield, skirting the edge of a device that's ready to detonate.

'There it is!' says the man as soon as he catches a glimpse, between the turquoise of the sky and the off-white of the sand, of a low, square, burned cedar building. It looks like a piece of Lego abandoned on the beach.

That's when the rhythm of the air changes again: a beat starts that the man doesn't recognise.

As they push open the door to the Archive, the man has a sense that all of the three hundred and thirty-three days spent reckoning with himself, and all of the years before spent avoiding himself, have led him here.

He'll never know it, but at the very moment he makes a small bow to the young, white-shirted man who greets them at the entrance, the air swells with the rhythm of a heart he once knew like the back of his hand.

chapter
one

FIVE-YEAR-OLD SHŪICHI HELD ONTO his handle-bars with the conviction that he was about to set off on a grand adventure. His escape from his mother's surveillance had been planned with such precision that, if the woman did find out, she would see how extraordinarily intelligent her son was, as well as how exceptionally attentively he had been observing her.

Shūichi's five years bore down on the seat of a red bicycle with no pedals. And he had only one objective: to make his heart explode.

They lived in Kamakura, at the top of a hill that connected the neighbourhoods of Ōmachi and Komachi via a tunnel whose origins nobody knew. Most people called it the Concubine's Tunnel because, according to legend, a landowner had it built so he could meet his lover from the other side of the mountain. Others talked of an anti-aircraft refuge used by the Japanese army for communications equipment during the Second World War.

The slopes that led to the tunnel were steep on both sides, so if somebody ventured up there by chance, they would find themselves out of breath halfway up. Cycling up the hill was impossible, and the children who lived in the area would often race down it for the prize of a tangerine or a marble. A high-schooler who had played there during his childhood once decided to calculate the range, gravitational energy and the increase and decrease of speed depending on the rider's body mass, whether you started from standing or were pushed by a hand (in which case the elevation of the release was taken into account too). His conclusion was that it was better to know none of this and just enjoy it.

These races only ever took place on one side of

the tunnel; the other remained forbidden for two reasons, because the road veered suddenly left, then right, and because just as you came out of the tunnel you could see the gravestones in the little cemetery that was carved into the side of the mountain.

It was said that on summer nights the spirits of the dead burned in tiny flames and in the daytime fluttered in clusters of butterflies.

Shūichi was the right age to be afraid of ghosts but he wasn't. The only fear that controlled him was that his own heart, at any moment, might burst.

He was diagnosed at birth with a heart murmur, a slight arrhythmia. He was exasperated by his mother's attentive listening to the music of his chest every morning and night, as if, through the metal disc and two earpieces, a prophecy might emerge.

He wasn't allowed to run alongside trains, or go on the fairground rides in Yokohama. And he couldn't go to summer festivals at all because of the big drums and general noise.

'This is your heart,' his mother had explained to him dozens of times, drawing its shape in pencil on a piece of paper, 'and this is the little hole that, if

11

you run too fast or tire yourself out, will get bigger and bigger until it rips open.'

With each new explanation, she took a fresh sheet of paper from her desk. It was as if going over the genesis of the story together, scaring him, helped her somehow.

And that was precisely why Shūichi sat on the precipice of the descent, gripping his handlebars for his life.

He wanted to do the most dangerous thing in the world and see what happened.

The noise she let out when she saw the silhouette of her son on his bicycle was his starting pistol.

'*Shūichi!!!*'

He pushed off with his legs and lifted them into a V shape. The sky felt close.

As he descended at a speed he had never known, he imagined himself transforming into an arrow, the giant one, at least five times as tall as his mother, that he had seen hanging under the roof of the Tsurugaoka Hachimangū shrine at New Year.

'*Shūichi, stop!!!! Shūichiiiiiiiii!*'

Thirty-five years later, Shūichi could remember the day of the accident in minute detail. The thing he remembered most clearly was the deafening boom of his own heart.

But despite being able to recall every single moment of that day – the sensation of piercing the air as he flew down the hill, the tight grip of his hands around the handlebars, glimpsing the emerging nose of a white car and missing it by a whisper, the intense pain in his arm and shoulder as they smashed into a wall like the wing of a baby bird taking flight too soon, the blood on his knees and the gap between his teeth that changed his smile for two years – his mother denied it ever happened.

'I think you probably imagined it.'

Shūichi got the same response when he asked about the time his precious sketchbook fell into the Nameri river; when his father smashed his bow in a fit of rage; when the cat was crushed under a tide of tools in the earthquake; even when they left his teddy bear, Loretto, on the train on that tragic trip to Kagoshima.

Shūichi recounted the painful memories to his mother: the accidents, the long episodes of childhood torment that he had held in; but she, without exception, denied them. The bear was just at home when they went on holiday and, indeed, on their return, there he was on the bed, more peaceful and sweeter than before; the sketchbook must still be buried somewhere in his room; and the bow? It was out on the porch, all in one piece!

'You replaced them all with new ones a few days after,' Shūichi accused her, 'and the cat was never seen again.'

'He was probably frightened by the earthquake. That cat loved exploring; I'm sure he just went to live somewhere else.'

But Shūichi could have sworn he'd seen the cat's mangled corpse under the brooms in the closet, his mother crying as she picked the boy up and carried him into the living room. She had turned on the TV, given him a hug, then slipped away to clean up.

'But I saw him,' he was animated. 'I saw you bury him in the garden.'

'You have always seen incredible things, Shūichi. This gift is what makes you who you are.'

The calmness with which she denied things confused him. How was it possible that Shūichi had never cried, that his love had been reciprocated every time he had given it? The world had seemed like a miracle ever since he was a child.

'And what about all these scars on my shoulders and knees?'

'I told you: you got them when you were older. How it happened I don't know. It was after you moved out.'

'But I remember flying down that hill on my bike, hitting the wall, missing the car by a matter of millimetres . . .'

'You must have dreamed it,' she interrupted him. 'As a child you loved plants, salted *onigiri* and picture books. You spent hours drawing windows and landscapes.'

Usually, the third time she denied things, Shūichi let it go. He would try again, though, every so often, incapable of giving up.

The last time he asked his mother about the bicycle accident, he was thirty-eight and she was seventy-five. On that day, too, she smiled patiently: 'Shūichi, you had a wonderful childhood. You saved up enough happiness that it should get you through adulthood too.'

Then what happened, happened, and everyone agreed that, for a while, happiness wouldn't be mentioned.

The speed of Shūichi's heartbeat as he went down (or imagined going down) the hill on his bike from the mouth of the tunnel

The heart of a five-year-old beats between seventy-five and a hundred and fifteen times a minute. The heart of an old man slows down to sixty. If you live a good life, your heart will complete a journey of three billion beats.

When it stops, it will have played a tune seventy or eighty years long and nobody will have paid it much attention. Apart from at certain times, like during a visit to the doctor's, at the end of a race, or after making love. Or on one of those rare occasions when you experience an irrational and desperate need to know that everything is OK and you place the palm of your hand on your chest.

On the descent, Shūichi's heart might have reached, at maximum, a hundred and eighty beats per minute. But if he had stayed in his bedroom curled up with Loretto the bear, and intensely imagined going down the hill, his heart might have reached almost the same rate.

The child who, on that day, *maybe* had a near miss with a car and *maybe* smashed into the wall of a house was now forty and walking up the road in the other direction.

It was autumn and little piles of leaves amassed along the sides of the Concubine's Tunnel.

From both hypotheses, which shared the sole certainty of having been five years old and in possession of a bicycle and a heart, a life had unfurled that was initially tranquil and, after thirty, quite complicated.

Shūichi blamed the tortuousness of his adult life on his yielding nature. He had agreed to mix with the world, had fallen in love with a woman, and had uttered, with surprising ease, a large number of yeses.

At forty, he was still undecided about whether to consider that period a mistake or the kind of fortune that strikes once in a lifetime.

Shūichi arrived in front of his childhood home,
breathless and with his heart beating fast in his chest.
He noted that the little gate was ajar and wondered
whether, in the three weeks the house had been empty,
a wild animal might have made its home in the garden.

There was a ripple of sadness as he realised he'd
never reached the door without his mother shouting
a welcome from inside.

It was only when he couldn't get his key in the
lock that he discarded the animal theory. Someone
must have forced open the door, leaving half a key
in there.

The lock incident was resolved in a day. Shūichi
called the emergency locksmith and reported it to
the police.

But the sense of intrusion left him unsettled. Who
would have tried to sneak into the house? And, more
importantly, who had a key? As far as he knew, only
two keys had been cut: one for the lady next door,
and one for him.

Three weeks had passed since his mother's funeral.
Shūichi had spent the time quickly restructuring the

map of his relationships, routines and work commitments and, after twelve years in Tōkyō, moved back to Kamakura. He planned to renovate his childhood home and sell it or rent it.

He knew that he would only be able to get rid of things by putting himself in the shoes of someone who didn't know the house. Having no memory made people more determined and capable.

He called a workman, not because he couldn't do it alone, but because having a stranger beside him as he dismantled the house would help him to look at it through neutral eyes.

It was exhausting. There were thousands, tens of thousands, of things. He was bewildered by the unwavering faith his mother had in objects. It was like she believed that they somehow made their life better.

Shūichi started by collecting everything that signified daily life: leftovers, detergents, towels, medicines. He even threw away essential items, convinced that if he made one exception he wouldn't be able to part with anything. He gathered up the things that belonged to his mother, sealed them in big, numbered boxes and put them in the garage. The car, unused for years, was sold.

In two days, with the workman's help, he pulled the paper off the walls in all the rooms, weakening the smell of ripe apple that defined his childhood memories. He then replaced the bathroom and kitchen, changed the tatami mats, got fresh parquet laid, and installed new shutters.

Every day felt like the day the house would change, the day the excess and the memories would be dismantled definitively. But the days passed and the work went on.

Sometimes, Shūichi thought he saw his mother. One afternoon, she was in the kitchen, aged around fifty, putting away a pan she used each year to begin the preparation of the *umeboshi*; one evening, as an old lady, holding onto the wall in the hallway on her way to the bathroom; and once in the garden, one summer when she was young and pushing him on the rope swing with its wooden seat, which she had hung from the branch of an oak tree on her own.

In those moments, Shūichi picked up his sketch-book, sat down on the porch and drew her exactly as he saw her: smiling and always, inexplicably, calm.

He had always trusted his pencil and, above all, his ability to see what had once been and no longer was.

In those days, going up and down the road of the Concubine's Tunnel, Shūichi sensed that someone was watching him. He turned around a couple of times but there was no one there.

Then, one Sunday, two weeks after his arrival, he passed the cemetery and scrutinised the house from afar. Assessing it as if for the first time, he found it in good shape, but still slightly too familiar. Repainting the external walls, he thought, could work. He realised only then what he was really trying to do: turn the house into something so unfamiliar that he could let it go.

That was when he noticed a shadow in front of the door.

He stood still. He followed the figure with his gaze as it wandered around the house. It approached the windows from the outside; it seemed to be looking for an entrance.

Shūichi did nothing. He moved just close enough to be able to see that the shadow belonged to a boy and that the boy knew the house well.

When he saw the boy come out of the garage with one of his mother's old watering cans and then hurry into the tunnel carrying it along with a bag full of books and trinkets, Shūichi started to make his way up the hill.

He got to the entrance to the tunnel and looked in, but the boy had disappeared.

As a young man, Shūichi used to go down to the sea at dawn, his surfboard attached to the side rack of his bike, Mount Fuji rising behind the Inamuragasa-ki promontory to the west. He always imagined that the sea gave birth to the mountain every morning. The only way he could describe the feeling of getting into the water with his board under his arm and that immense mountain ahead was to say that he couldn't find the words.

Even as an adult, living in Tōkyō, if he had a free weekend he would come back to Kamakura and spend Saturday and Sunday wandering around temples, sitting on the beach, and drawing. Sometimes he brought his bike and pedalled out to Enoshima island, climbed to the top and let himself be absorbed by the bustle of tourists and the horizon.

On his return, his mother would wait for him in the garden with the same apprehension she used to have when he was a child and she checked his heartbeat. 'How was the sea today?' she'd ask. Then she'd hold his wrist and ask him if he was out of breath. 'Yes, but it's just from the hill,' he answered every time, and every time she looked unconvinced.

At eighteen, Shūichi started art school in Tōkyō. To avoid paying rent, he commuted to and from Kamakura. Leaving the station and seeing the blue-grey mountains on his way home more than made up for the early mornings and late evenings.

Even though they were living in the same house, his schedule meant Shūichi and his mother rarely crossed paths. They tried to renew their routines at long intervals: breakfasts that were more like lunches, chatting late into the night under the *kotatsu*, *yuzu* tea to soothe non-existent sore throats.

Their intimacy, sown with such meticulous care at the beginning, produced such an abundance of flowers and fruit over the years that it no longer required much effort.

Shūichi owed her so much. Above all, he owed her the work that coloured his days: his career as an illustrator. His mother had known to value his wide-open gaze that, ever since he was a boy, saw cats as secret messengers, windows as magical portals and insects that joyfully came out in summer as invaders from other planets. She had believed in him even when nothing suggested he deserved it.

Since her passing, something in Shūichi had been extinguished. He wouldn't have been able to put it into words, but another knot in the rope that kept him tied to the world had come loose.

His mother was a cheerful woman. She struggled to hold on to anger; it melted into a constant fear that something might happen to Shūichi. But when she suffered, she became bolder. After her husband's sudden death fifteen years earlier, she wore the same mourning kimono for a week, and didn't even take the bin out. When Shūichi went round to see her days later, he could smell it from the front door. Banana skins and milk: his mother had eaten nothing else since the morning of the funeral.

His strongest memory of her, though, was the faith she had in everyone. If ever she couldn't find positive qualities, she would invent them. Ever since he was young, she had showed Shūichi that there was always a way to love people. She didn't ignore their faults, but she didn't load herself up with the weight of nasty words either. 'Imagine how much they already suffer just by being with themselves!' she'd say. Even commenting on the most atrocious crimes, his mother explained that it was possible to put someone in prison without having to hate them. It was a relief for Shūichi to discover that he could respect people who made mistakes too.

This, more than anything else she said, had profoundly influenced him.

So now, thinking of the boy burglar, rather than feeling angry, Shūichi was curious to find out what on earth a young boy was planning to do with an old watering can, his mother's stained apron and a chipped cup.

He soon discovered that the little robbery was repeated every afternoon, when the boy was on his way home from school and Shūichi had just gone out.

doki doki

'I want to die here,' whispered the older boy.

'Why here?' the younger boy asked.

He sat down next to him on the riverbank.

'Because here I know the names of all the things.'

'All of them?'

'Yes, all of them. If I ask my grandma the name of an insect, she always knows it. She even knows how swallows make their nests and why there are holes in acorns.'

'Why are there holes in acorns?'

'Because larvae live inside them. They're called *zō-mushi*, elephant-bugs, because they have a really long trunk like elephants.'

The older boy got up and pulled a handful of acorns out of his pocket.

'Also, I know all the best places around here to collect them.'

He placed one that was full of holes in his hand and showed the younger boy. Then he started whispering again: 'I want to die here, definitely.'

The younger boy looked at the acorn in silence.

'So that when I'm reborn like the Buddha as a stone, an acorn, or even a larva, I'll know my way around. I'll always be able to find my way home, because around here I know the name of all the things.'

He said it just like that: I'll know my way around; I'll be reborn as an acorn or a larva. Or maybe he said a squirrel or a leaf?

The younger boy wanted to object; to say something like, if you really have to be reborn as something else, wouldn't it be better to be a superhero or a dinosaur or an insect? In fact, if he could squeeze in anywhere, he would like to be reborn in the tiny hole next to the handle of his bedroom door, which he had made himself, in secret, with a fork.

Life is a succession of shipwrecks.

The island we wash up on, the state of our ship, the life raft, our arms, the only objects remaining from our concluded life: everything becomes important. Because upon arrival on the beach, whatever the existence that preceded it was like, it is now memory.

No matter how much pain we have accumulated, life begins again.

'A shipwreck?'

The pane of glass looked out over the intersection of tracks of the Chūo Line and a bit further down, tiny heads bustled across a zebra crossing. Then the traffic lights turned red and the little blobs of colour all stopped at the edge.

Shūichi nodded. 'Yes, a shipwreck,' he mumbled, staring at the crossing.

'But the protagonist then has some encounters, I presume . . .'

'No, he gets shipwrecked and that's it.'

Shūichi turns to the man sitting behind the desk at the far end of the room. He recognises his disoriented expression and that way of speaking, the loosening of every word, which happened whenever they started talking about a new book and the editor was afraid of not getting it.

'And so . . . it's a survival story?'

'You could say that.'

'Got it.'

Shūichi took all of Tōkyō in. It was a bright morning, the wreck of an entire city was beneath his feet, who knows how many people were struggling to stay afloat. And yet the blue of the sky made it look so tranquil.

'And so, what happens on this island?'

'Nothing,' Shūichi responded, walking towards the desk. He pulled out the chair and sat down, his elbows on his satchel. The editor leaned all his weight on to the back of his chair.

'Nothing? Nothing happens?'

'Nothing. He goes for a walk and gets a feel for

the place. What animals live there, what plants. He grapples a bit with the solitude, I'd say, if we really must find a meaning.'

'A meaning . . .'

'Because adults need meanings, right?'

'I suppose so.'

'It's different for children. They find meaning while they're doing things, not before or after.'

The editor sighed.

Shūichi got up and turned to the window just as the orange Chūo train passed through Kanda Station and sped towards Tōkyō-eki. He imagined it cutting through not air but water and the immense orange waves that would engulf the city. The smell of citrus filled Shūichi's nostrils and he closed his eyes.

'A shipwreck, then . . .'

'Yes, Ishii-san, a shipwreck.'

Leaving the publisher's office, Shūichi took the stairs rather than the lift. Through the windows, he glimpsed the passing of a train and a flock of crows flying high in the air.

As he descended the thirty-two floors, he thought about the boy stealing from the house every day.

He wondered what he might have taken from the garage that afternoon. A frying pan, another picture book, maybe a gardening tool.

He smiled, imagining his face on finding the gift.

chapter

two

TO CAPTURE A MOONFISH, YOU need an ink-black seabed and a handful of starfish.

To pull up a swordfish, you need a thick net and a sheath.

To hook a dogfish, you need a lead and a lot of cuddles.

And to catch a boy-fish? To seize his heart (and do it no harm), what do you need?

One week earlier, Shūichi woke in the middle of the night. He was out of breath. He was breathing as if he had just run up the hill at full speed.

He had dreamed he was six again and doing the final recital at kindergarten. All the children around him were wearing red, in outfits made with a lot of help from their teachers. Sticky discs arranged into words of thanks decorated the room; their hats were constructed from strips of cardboard with elastic bands tying the ends together. On the floor under his feet were bits of Sellotape and glitter. They had been running through the steps of the dance for a long time; the music was a pop song with the lyrics rewritten to make it about gratitude, six years of friendship, the joy of new meetings that would alter their horizons once again. Indeed, after that day, the diaspora would begin: based on their home address, the children would be distributed into the three primary schools in a ten-kilometre radius of Kamakura station. It would happen in April when the cherry blossom was in bloom.

Shūichi was waiting for his mother. In the meantime, the parents of his classmates looked on with the unease of adults in a child-sized world; they sat on the floor, chatting quietly. His mother, usually early, was late. When, from behind the curtain, he finally saw her appear with her handbag on her arm,

36

THE LIBRARY OF HEARTBEATS

her kimono wrapped around her tiny figure, her eyes red, makeup thick, and lip swollen, Shūichi immediately knew something bad had happened.

His mother smiled for the entire duration of the recital. She remained still, on folded knees, as Shūichi tried his best not to imagine anything.

The thing that periodically revisited him in his dreams as an adult, however, wasn't the recital, but the journey home, his mother's slight limp as they walked along the dark streets of Kamakura, and bedtime when Shūichi pretended to go to sleep but, stock-still behind the door, spied on her as she removed her makeup in front of the mirror. He would remember her deathly slow movements as she spread the cream over her face and the strange magic when, instead of returning to white, the cotton wool left colour in its wake. Midnight blue and carnation red.

In the dream, the image was engulfed by the black roller waves of Shūichi's terror, like a petroleum tsunami devouring his mother's face, sliding down her neck, twisting over her shoulder, falling like dark liquid onto her chest, and eventually liquefying her.

Shūichi had no idea if that day really happened,

37

or if the memory came from a documentary on TV, or rumours about Koda-san, the wife of the neighbour, who, after years of violence, had reported her husband to the police. Shūichi never asked his mother if it really happened. Not because he was frightened she would deny it, but that she wouldn't.

Deep down, Shūichi believed that if you didn't talk about things, they came back to you in your dreams.

That night, like every night, Shūichi put a hand on his heart, got up, and drank a glass of water.

Back in bed, he scoured his mind for an image that would calm him down. Among many, for reasons he didn't understand, was the image of the mysterious boy whose name he didn't know. He had seen him walk past the garden that morning, before seven, dawdling with his rucksack on his back and eyes squinting into the sun. They were curious, intelligent eyes.

The tenderness Shūichi had experienced gave him joy and at the same time made him anxious.

But he decided, this time, to ignore the latter.

Years later, he would be able to see that this decision marked the beginning of his third life.

For a week, Shūichi let himself be spied on by the boy, and for a week, he spied back.

When one of them was sitting behind his desk at school, the other sketched at his drawing board, and in the afternoons, at a distance, they met.

They took it in turns. Shūichi pretended to be the most distracted person in the world: he didn't notice the shadow that stretched in front of his house at sunset; he accidentally left the door ajar when he went out, the garage wide open to let the fresh air in. Sometimes, on his way down to the city, he glimpsed the boy's reflection in the glass of a window; caught him, out of the corner of his eye, bundled up between the headstones in the cemetery, or leaning against the fence by the bridge that crossed the Nameri river which marked, on the Komachi side, the end of the road from the Concubine's Tunnel.

Once, during a downpour, they crossed paths in the narrow darkness of the tunnel and the roar of the rain drowned out the sound of their footsteps. The boy stubbornly stared at his own feet and Shūichi did the same, apart from a split second when they both turned to look at each other: a momentary lag saved them from exposure.

39

But Shūichi had an enormous advantage. He knew that, once he got home, he would be able to calmly study the boy. He had installed a camera, hidden among the boxes at the back of the garage on top of all the old kitchen equipment.

He would never normally have done such a thing, for no reason other than the lack of emotion that dragged him through the world. But his curiosity to know who this child was and what relationship he had with his mother's house was heightened by the fact that the things the boy took away each afternoon were worth so little. Shūichi found himself incapable of finding the indifference he was used to protecting himself with.

Later that evening, he pulled the packaging off his bentō box, stuck his wooden chopsticks into a cloud of white rice, soy sauce, and chicken croquettes, switched on his computer and watched the footage that he had recorded from two in the afternoon until six.

On the tapes, where everything was tinged with the bluish hues of distant mountains, the boy emptied the boxes, cutting the packing tape with the tip of a pencil, and timidly sorting through them. He took

objects out with care and slipped some of them into
a large cotton bag. He looked at his watch regularly,
as if to remind himself that time was passing.

Shūichi saw that the boy was searching for something, but it seemed that as he searched, he became
absorbed by the objects that were gathered there.

It seemed like, in that sea of bric-a-brac, everything
was speaking to the boy.

Seeing the boy handling those objects with an emotion that Shūichi had worked hard to cordon off made
the memories come flooding back.

He returned in his mind to the day of his mother's
death: he noticed only now the schoolbooks that,
years after retirement, had found their way back onto
the living-room table. He saw the pantry full of flour,
yeast and chocolate like when he was still living at
home. His mother didn't have a sweet tooth; there
was no way she had bought all that for herself.

With a firm hand, he reopened, one by one, all
of the rooms in his memory. In the hallway he saw
the world map he'd been so fascinated by as a child
('The world is big, Shūichi, travel! Look how much
space there is on the planet! Remember that when

41

a place is too small for you, you can always leave. Leaving doesn't have to be a bad thing.'); he spotted the games he had sealed up two years earlier repositioned in view, the bicycle back in the garden.

He had noticed all these strange details when he and the workman were dismantling the house, but he had pushed down the questions as they came up. His mother was dead now, what did it matter? And, anyway, where was the sense in condemning yourself to curiosity with no answers?

Shūichi had always hated suspense; it was too disruptive. He was obsessive, and until he knew how a story ended, he couldn't let it go. He started books with a forced slowness, choosing ones where each paragraph could satisfy him without making him hungry to know what happened next. Often, to release the pressure, he withdrew from the race before the end. He looked up the plot of films and TV series. He found it frustrating that he couldn't do the same with people, or with life's big decisions.

The new, for Shūichi, was an unbearable risk.

The character for 'new' and how it grew, over the years, inside Shūichi

'The *kanji* for *shin* 新, new, is the combination of the characters 辛, 木 and 斤,' said his mother, drawing them on the whiteboard in the living room.

She had brought it home when the school she taught at closed for renovation. She thought it would be useful to have a whiteboard at home to practise on.

辛 was a sort of 'big needle with a handle', an instrument Shūichi struggled to imagine. In the end, after a long and futile search, he understood it as a sort of little arrow. Looking at it confirmed this: the shaft, the fletching, the nock.

His mother explained to him that an arrow was once fired to select the tree (木) to cut down for making sacred objects like funeral tablets.

As she sketched the story out with a little piece of chalk, Shūichi imagined men in ancient China gripping onto the formless object and hurling it into the air to identify the chosen tree, then felling that tree with an axe (斤). He discovered that the practice of firing an arrow was ancient and that the sacred rite was also used to decide where to start the construction of important buildings.

'See, Shūichi, the whole ritual is wrapped up in this *kanji*.'

The boy remembered how his mother's voice rose, swelling with her primary-school-teacher enthusiasm. He could see her explaining that cutting down that particular tree, selected in a complex ritual performed not by men but by divine will, had, over time, become synonymous with 'new beginnings, novelty'.

'And that's why,' she concluded, 'still today we use 新 to mean something new.'

Shūichi was fascinated by the story, and by the extraordinary transformation he had just witnessed in his mother: she was born to teach. If he was jealous of anything as a child, it was the time she spent at school with her pupils.

At ten, at twenty, at forty years old, Shūichi was still sure that new things had something to do with destiny: an arrow to choose a tree, an axe to chop it down, and, most importantly, something big and sacred to build with the wood.

Novelty, for Shūichi, had always encompassed faith, construction and chance.

The idea of the gift came to Shūichi because he knew that you could only catch a boy-fish with little pieces of itself.

He had spent hours drawing it. He started slowly, planning a single sketch in the centre of the page. But then it grew spontaneously, like an avocado plant from the stone. It happened just as he overcame his fear of the nonsensical familiarity (he knew for certain he had never met him before) that he felt towards the boy. There was a likeness he couldn't explain, and it made Shūichi feel exposed. But he knew how to keep this fear at bay, so he picked up his pencil and a piece of paper.

When he finished his first drawing, he wanted to continue. He hesitated before starting the second, but only because he knew that once he had drawn something, he would never forget it.

As it got dark, he turned on his work lamp and started the third.

And that's how Shūichi completed a character study: an entire page of twenty-four vignettes that he first sketched out in pencil, then painted in watercolour. It was the boy, his features defined with the precision of a professional who knows not only how to perfectly capture the lines of a face but also the indistinct point where the soul nests, bringing everything together. He had depicted him in little spheres, where his face appeared joyful, then surprised, then alert; here bent over a box, there in profile with a rucksack on his back, here as he chewed his nails, there as he sneezed.

When Shūichi finished, it was late into the night. It had been years since he had been so absorbed by drawing that he forgot to eat dinner. He took his stamp from the drawer, pressed it into the little cushion of red ink and placed his seal in the bottom right-hand corner of the page. He went to bed feeling content, wondering about the best way to give it to the boy.

He had no idea how the child would react, but he knew it probably wouldn't be how he expected.

At least not at first.

He accepted the risk.

The next day, he laid the sheet in full view in the garage, turned off the camera and headed towards the station.

He had a meeting in Tōkyō with his editor. He was going to talk to him about the comic book he'd been working on for ages, a dream he'd had, and a child in a shipwreck.

Why Shūichi believed you could only catch a boy-fish with little pieces of itself

It was because of a story Shūichi had read when he was a child.

The story was about the people who lived in a town far away, who travelled in search of a cure for a bizarre illness that afflicted men, women, young and old alike.

Inside each person's body, almost daily, little holes started to form: holes as wide as the circumference of a pencil and as deep as its point. For the whole of their lives, these little holes closed and opened ceaselessly. They were filled every so often when the people encountered something that made them happy. But it wasn't forever and, apart from a few mysterious cases, those holes, even the ones that closed, always opened up again.

After decades of searching, the people arrived at the resting place of a Buddhist monk. They asked

49

him if he knew how to fill up all these little holes once and for all, and the old sage explained that the only thing that could heal them was not something new and separate from themselves, but 'something that was truly part of you from the beginning'. That was the only way they could repair themselves once and for all. Glass was repaired with glass, wool with wool, flesh with flesh.

In the same way, every authentic feeling had to start and end with itself: joy had to be independent from the world's response; happiness couldn't depend on anyone else.

Everything, essentially, was in seeking outside what was already inside.

The first step, however, was the most complicated: understanding what we have inside.

Shūichi couldn't remember how the story ended, whether the little holes became scars, or whether those people ever went home. Nor did he know the title of the story because he didn't look for it. He didn't want to see it, in case he had remembered it wrong.

When Shūichi got home, he saw that nothing had been taken.

There was no sign of the boy or the drawing in the garage. He probably got scared, he thought, and regretted turning off the camera and putting the sheet of paper in full view.

The boy didn't come in the days that followed either.

After a week of absence, Shūichi was tempted to go and look for him, but he told himself it was best to let things play out.

The truth was that even if the boy didn't come back voluntarily, Kamakura was so small that within a matter of days they would probably bump into one another at the supermarket, in the queue in front of a shrine, or sitting at neighbouring tables in Starbucks. Apart from the tourists, you always saw the same people in that town.

Shūichi was wrong; more than two weeks passed and when Shūichi saw him, the boy was standing on the Tōshoji Bridge in a strange position.

Seeing the boy's tense face and contracted jaw, Shūichi wondered for a second if he might be the reason for the boy's trembling.

But the boy hadn't even clocked the man's presence. His heart was pounding, but it wasn't because of Shūichi.

It was because he had been running away from two bullies, who were also there on the bridge.

It was probably the end of an episode that started at school and had been dragged all the way here.

It didn't look like it was the first time. Shūichi perceived a sort of rituality that tormentors and victim were equally used to.

'Give it back,' the boy said in a strained voice.

'But why are you so slow?' taunted the shorter of the two.

The other laughed, fortifying the joke. All three were wearing the same uniform.

The boy looked more exhausted than humiliated. He moved towards them with great weariness.

Shūichi noticed only then that one of the two boys was holding something in his hand, waving it around in the air and dodging the boy every time he tried to get hold of it. When he lurched forward once again to take back what belonged to him, bored perhaps by the game, the shorter of the two boys threw something over the bridge's parapet, into the Nameri river. All three of them ran instinctively to look over the edge.

Shūichi also shot forward onto the bridge.

Surprised by the sound of his footsteps, the two boys turned towards the man who was now behind them. Unsure whether this adult was somehow related to the other boy and whether they were about to get into trouble, they ran. The sounds of their feet, their laughter and their leather rucksacks bumping on their backs floated through the air.

It was only then that the boy noticed Shūichi. He stood still, hurt.

Neither of them, this time, looked down at the floor.

'Quick, over here.'

Shūichi pointed to a staircase of large rocks leading from the right-hand side of the bridge down to the river. The steps were roughly cut and covered in moss and other plant life. They worked their way down cautiously, holding onto the stone wall.

The sheet of paper was lying on one of the flat stone slabs that made up the riverbed. It hadn't been washed away as, miraculously, the water was low that day.

'Stay here and hold this for me, please,' Shūichi said to the boy, passing him his own bag. 'Careful it doesn't get wet.'

Then he took off his shoes and socks, rolled up the bottoms of his trousers and, with a few small hops, reached the paper. He picked it up, turned towards the boy smiling, and held it in the air like a trophy.

'Just the edge is wet. If you put it out in the sun, it will dry really quickly,' he said. 'It might crinkle a little, but luckily it's thick paper.'

That's when Shūichi recognised it. It was the twenty-four portraits he had drawn: the character study.

'Are you going to tell me off?' asked the boy, once they were back on the bridge. 'Are you going to tell my mother?'

'I don't know your mother,' Shūichi responded. 'But I would like to know why you've taken so many things that belonged to mine.'

He didn't say *steal*: he sensed that there were deeper reasons behind the thefts. 'Don't judge what you don't know,' was his mother's motto.

The boy was silent.

'I'm curious, that's all.'

'There were things in there that were mine too,' the boy finally responded, in a tone that to Shūichi's ear betrayed resentment. He seemed to take offence to something he hadn't yet explained.

'Couldn't you have told me? I would have helped you look for them . . .'

'You were destroying Mrs Ōno's house; I was scared you were going to throw everything away.'

'I wasn't *destroying* the house: I was just *renovating* it.' Shūichi felt defensive.

The boy remained serious, unconvinced.

'Anyway, you only had to knock on the door and tell me.'

Shūichi repeated this sentence, but halfway through he could already foresee the end. The minds of children reasoned in a completely different way.

If the child did not trust adults, he surely had good reason for it.

'So, did you know my mother, Mrs Ōno, for long?'

'She helped me with school.'

Shūichi nodded. 'Come to the house so you can explain properly, and we'll look for your things.'

The boy didn't respond but followed him until they settled into the same pace.

'Where do you live?'

'There.'

His finger rested on the opening of a narrow road, parallel to the one that led to the Concubine's Tunnel, which also climbed steeply up the mountain. That was the way to climb up to the Yakumo-jinja shrine.

'What's your name?'

'Kenta.'

'Kenta . . .'

The boy stuffed his hand into his pocket and pulled something out. He held his palm out to Shūichi.

'What is it?'

The boy looked him in the eye for a moment,

56

then lowered his gaze onto the little piece of metal. 'Mrs Ōno gave it to me on my birthday.'

Shūichi understood.

'It was broken,' he said. 'I didn't steal it.'

'I believe you.'

It was just like his mother to give such an absurd gift to a child on their birthday. To give an object, but really be giving a concept: the key to the house, and, with it, her complete trust.

doki doki

'How old are you?'

'Six. You?'

'Eight, I'm going into year three. This year I'm gonna learn a ton of *kanji*. Like the one for *station* and the one for *swim* . . . which is like the one for *water* but harder.'

'I still can't write. I'm no good.'

'Writing is awesome!' the older boy exclaimed.

'Why?'

'Because you can stop things.'

The younger boy's face darkened. He didn't understand, and when he didn't understand, he felt sad.

'What do you mean?'

'People talk too fast and I forget everything, but when I write it down, I can remember it.'

'But even if you can't remember it, it's OK.'

Some things are nice to remember forever.'

58

There were only part-time teachers running the afternoon club activities that year: young and inexperienced teachers who weren't very motivated.

Kenta's parents paid the afternoon fees, but the boy was free to go home if he wanted to. It was tough being eight: school, homework, the classmates with their extraordinary memory for other people's mistakes. Free time was tiring too.

So Kenta left school and wandered, lost in his imagination, sometimes talking out loud, singing softly, kicking the air. He leaned over the edge of the Tōshoji Bridge, dropped sticks and stones he'd gathered into the water, and every now and then sat on a bench to read manga.

He didn't do badly at school, but didn't make much effort either. The worst thing, though, according to Mrs Ōno, was that he didn't have fun:

'If you don't have fun at school, where do you think happiness will come from?'

As Shūichi listened to Kenta, he filled the gaps in the boy's disjointed phrases with his own imagination. He talked about his mornings at school, his afternoons spent with Mrs Ōno, life at home with his parents, a trip he had gone on to a farm in Chiba two months ago; he made the omissions and leaps typical of children, whose logic is based primarily on feeling. So although Shūichi didn't understand everything he was trying to say and the details into which he would suddenly dive, he didn't ask questions. He knew that, depending on the intensity of the emotion, children reversed the logic of words: he just had to wait.

But what moved him most was hearing the boy speak: the sound of his voice, the slight stutter that slowed certain words. Perhaps that was why he couldn't concentrate fully. And what were those palpitations he could feel?

Shūichi pushed the reasons away.

'Are you hungry?' he interrupted when Kenta also looked lost.

'Yeah . . . but I guess you've also thrown out Mrs Ōno's chocolate.'

Shūichi smiled at Kenta's constant accusations. He hadn't forgiven him for turning the house over. When he learned that the boy had been there almost every day for over a year, he understood why.

What really amazed him, though, was that his mother had never mentioned this child. Why hadn't she talked to him about Kenta?

'There's no chocolate, but I can make pancakes if you want. Do you like pancakes?'

'Do you have strawberry jam?'

'I don't think so.'

'Peach?'

'No.'

'Honey?'

'I see you're not easy to please,' Shūichi smiled.

'If you're going to do something, you have to do it properly.'

The echo of those words, uttered with the exact intonation of his mother, filled the kitchen, then fell, like a glass of water slipped from a hand.

'Shall we go to the shops?'

As the boy got his jacket and they planned their

trip – which side of the mountain they would walk down, which shops they would go to – and Kenta reeled off the list of snacks they wanted, seeming to already trust him completely, Shūichi wondered what point of their story they were at: the beginning, the middle, or the end. And he was scared that he would always be missing too many elements to understand. 'Tell me from the beginning, if you can . . .' he wanted to say.

But he knew that a story can begin anywhere, and that sooner or later you find out where it ends.

It took more than a week to find out exactly how his mother and the boy had met.

It was autumn. Shūichi noted that important things always seemed to happen in autumn.

They had met at the start of the road that led to the Concubine's Tunnel, where the path, on which perched the two-storey house where the boy lived, branched off and arched up the mountain. Kenta's parents didn't get on: the child had spent a couple of years begging them for a sibling, and then stopped. Now he would be happy if, instead of fighting, they just learned to live in silence.

That day, Mrs Ōno had started walking up the hill on her way home from the market when her bag of fruit split. Kenta saw three apples rolling down the road: one came to a halt against the steps of a house, another stopped not far from his feet, and the third was still rolling.

Kenta quickly collected up the fruits and ran to catch up with her.

'Apples?' asked Shūichi.

'Apples,' Kenta answered.

'And then?'

And then she asked him what year he was in, what he was studying, whether he liked it, and what exactly he didn't like and why. Mrs Ōno asked a lot of questions.

Kenta had mentioned then that *kanji* looked like insects, and that they seemed to just slip through his fingers, so she invited him round for a snack and to see whether, together, they could figure out a way to catch them.

'Because they're wonderful, you know?' she had said. The fact that those insects were tricky to catch, and even trickier to keep hold of, just meant they were precious, alive and worth all the hard work.

63

Mrs Ōno managed to see the *kanji* as he saw them: creatures with a thousand legs and antennae and an incredible aptitude for camouflage. This, more than anything else – more than the fruit and seed cakes that would come later, more than the hot chocolate with pieces of real chocolate in, and even more than all the other special treats that only children could imagine – won him over. The house did the rest, which seemed to embrace him every time he arrived in front of it.

The more Shūichi listened to Kenta, the more he saw that a part of his mother had been deposited in this boy. He knew the risk he was running, but the joy of hearing her so alive in the boy's words gave him such a sense of well-being that Shūichi was incapable of defending himself.

After the apples incident, Kenta continued, they ended up, almost by chance, meeting every afternoon. The very next day, on the table of the living room where he had eaten pieces of apple with acacia honey the day before, the boy found a pile of third-grade books.

'If I had a question, she answered it, and she explained it much better than the teachers at school.

64

I understood straightaway and I never felt stupid,' he said.

For Kenta, the most extraordinary thing about Mrs Ōno was that if she didn't know something, she admitted it: 'I'm not sure, you know', 'Do you know, I can't remember', she'd laugh, and she'd throw herself, along with him, into finding out, with a joy that was even greater than when she knew the answer from the start.

The old lady never told him to come and see her every afternoon, but he could tell she was expecting him. The scent of cakes, pancakes, fruit compote and cream *dorayaki* enveloped the house and Kenta could smell it from the bottom of the road.

He didn't say as much to Shūichi, but even now that Mrs Ōno was gone, after school, instead of running to her house to have a snack and tell her about his day, he ran from his classmates and wandered the streets until his parents got home from work; even now, sometimes, he could almost smell the sugar and jam in the air, and when he walked up there and found the door closed, he felt a pain he didn't know where to put, if not there in the corner of his heart that was home to the old lady who had taught him the wonderful stories of the *kanji*, the order in which the lines had to be drawn, and was always baking something new, just for him.

Nobody had ever paid Kenta that much attention.

When Kenta's story was finished, Shūichi was sure that he could have gone on for days.

Summarising it was too simple: his mother had welcomed in a boy who looked lost, encouraged him to study and made him food; he learned, had fun, gave her some company. She made the boy happy; the boy made her happy.

But Shūichi felt there was something Kenta wasn't saying. He didn't know if it was to do with his mother, with the boy, or with something the boy knew about Shūichi.

How much exactly had his mother told Kenta about her life? Which parts of Shūichi's story did he know? And why had his mother never mentioned this boy?

If there was a secret, it would come out with time.

'Did you like the drawing I did for you?'

The boy nodded. 'But they ruined it.'

'It doesn't matter. If you want, I can do another one.'

After finding them in the garage, Kenta had stared at those drawings, enraptured. He had put the sheet of paper in his school bag, and had opened it secretly at school, in the corridor, in class, in the bathroom, between the pages of a textbook on his desk. He never took the whole thing out, though, keeping it in the shadows. That was what had attracted the attention of the two boys.

'At your age, you don't need to show people what you have.' It was the first rule of earning people's disinterest, of being left in peace.

In reality, Shūichi knew that to succeed in that intention, you needed to thicken the membrane that separated you from the world, and to quiet the joy of being alive. Beautiful things, when not spoken aloud, decayed. Was it worth it? After forty years, he still wasn't sure.

He opted to stay quiet.

LAURA IMAI MESSINA

One day, however, he found a list in Kenta's hand-writing between the pages of one of the textbooks disinterred from the garage. The list contained all the techniques he planned to use to face his eighth year. That's when Shūichi understood that he and the child were the same.

Kenta's list for facing his
eighth year

1. To turn down the volume of the world: put in earphones.
2. To make things less important: don't give them names (don't name the chair or the clock, or the boy in your class).
3. To see nothing: stare at a light bulb (only for a few seconds until everything becomes a big yellow spot).
4. To not smell anything: breathe with your mouth, avoid eating (this way you also save your taste and don't get tempted by chips).

chapter
three

$\mathcal{S}$URFING WAS SHŪICHI'S FAVOURITE SPORT.
He knew that some people, in order to predict the frequency, power and height of the waves, would always study the currents, water temperature and landforms of the coast before getting in the water. He, however, was seduced by an instinctive drive to jump on a wave just in case it was a good one.

Kamakura never got much more than a modest ripple but, far from demotivating him, he found the small scale of it enticing. Surfing was made for him, he thought, because it challenged him: not so much in terms of the staying upright while everything moved underneath, but the patience of waiting for the perfect wave, and catching and riding the mediocre ones that came in the meantime.

Was this what he was choosing each time he got in the water?

In the calm of the Sagami Bay, the sea flat, surfers sitting on the beach, total inertia, came a wave. An unremarkable wave. And that was when Shūichi, without even considering the idea of waiting for a better one, jumped onto his board and started to paddle.

Kenta came into his life in the same way.

As did Sayaka.

You only had to go about ten metres from the road and you could look down at the tracks and see the tip of the platform, only officially accessible by going through the station which was much further along.

Shūichi loved that place: he felt like he was in the only spot in the world where you could secretly observe humanity, spying from under the tablecloth. He had always thought it was a special place; all the expectations in the world were concentrated on the platforms of train stations.

Enveloped by night, *Sararin* fish-and-sake restaurant defended itself with a red paper lamp and a triangle of window lit by a single trembling flame.

He went inside and sat down in the most sheltered corner. Shūichi imagined Kenta's surprise if he'd been faced with that menu and all the parts of the fish, their names, surnames, nicknames. The owner's daughter had designed it. She was now sixteen and attending art school: she wanted to become a *mangaka*. He remembered talking to her about it once and knowing just from her tone of voice that she would succeed. Shūichi thought that Kenta would like that place, would have liked talking to her.

He smiled. He realised this was how you know you care about someone: when you see them where they aren't. Kenta wasn't there, but Shūichi could see him beside him, laughing.

Shūichi had already drunk his third cup of sake. The edges of the bar were blurry, the flavour broken down into parts.

Sayaka was suddenly next to him and he wondered if he had called her or if she had come to his table by accident.

Only when she asked him, 'But do you really not remember me?' did Shūichi make a concerted effort to focus. He pinned down the wall, froze the table, arrested the glasses and signalled for her to be quiet.

He took hold of her arm, pressed his thumb to the inside of her wrist and, wrapping his other fingers around it, listened.

'Are you taking my heart rate?'

'Have I never done that?'

Sayaka shook her head.

'Well, that means we don't know each other very well,' Shūichi murmured, letting go of her wrist.

'I don't know how well is very well for you, but last time we met you told me you had nothing to give me.'

'I said that?'

'I have nothing to give you, you said. You said it exactly like that.'

'And I was sober . . . ?'

'Does it make a difference?'

'Perhaps not . . .'

They started again from the beginning. Shūichi went first.

She didn't say anything as she didn't want to stop him talking, but she already knew it all.

'I'm an illustrator, I make children's books.'

'A very successful one,' she added, smiling.

'Perhaps,' he responded.

'Don't be modest.'

Shūichi had won many prizes, and his work appeared in all the biggest newspapers and magazines. He even put on shows every now and then. But he wasn't being modest. Over the years, he had learned that the real joy of things resided in not revealing them, and feeling happy just because you know they're true.

'And do you like it?' Sayaka asked.

He wouldn't have known what else to do, he responded, but the truth was that Shūichi had continued doing that work for twenty years because he loved changing the form of things. Most of all, he liked the beginning, when he was starting to write a new book and would spend entire days in the library: he'd go in with a single word and come out with a forest of them. Then, in the days that followed, he'd write, noting down all the most interesting things he'd found. Estuaries formed; rivers widened.

All of his stories started like this, at the exact point where his interior life mixed with life outside, and he forgot what it meant to be only himself.

Once, during an interview, a journalist had told him that listening to him speak was like witnessing the Big Bang: it was astonishing how a single idea expanded, exploding into a supernova. 'It astounds me to think of all the strips you have drawn, each one full of hundreds of details, windows that open up onto new worlds, and that they all come from a single, tiny idea.' But, Shūichi corrected her, the hardest part was identifying the essence, circum-scribing the infinite hunger that every story has inside of it. There, in that division, was where he recognised himself.

That's why he kept the finished work but threw out all the drafts and sketches. They confused him, even if he was unsettled by the process of brushing away the scraps to leave the definitive form.

'And you?'

'I work with bodies; I prepare the dead for their final event.'

'Funerals . . .'

'I help those who remain to let them go. I wash the women's and men's bodies, make up their faces and dress them.'

Shūichi flattened his hand. 'Wait,' he said.

Sayaka waited.

'I remember you.'

Sayaka spoke and her voice brought the pungent smell of incense into the restaurant, the softness of the flowers that celebrated their own end as well as that of others, the rose-and-peony-scented creams she used to massage the bodies.

Shūichi listened attentively, and took his turn when she finished. He brought the smell of sharpened pencil shavings, the rough paper that lay in his sketchbooks, and the smooth, glossy pages of a just-printed book.

They brought into the ten square metres of the fish-and-sake restaurant the story of her brother, who was about to marry a woman who saw invisible colours in every person she met, and the story of his mother, the woman Shūichi knew and the woman she had been with others. She was both of them, he mumbled, and both of them were true.

They spoke quietly about how every mother, every father, every person you know is a constant betrayal. Which is the real person? Where does the woman who was just 'your mother' end? Which is the true one? The one *with* you or *without* you? They wondered what was more important: what we see, or what is off-limits to our hearts.

'And now there's this boy . . . It seems he spent every afternoon with my mother and I know nothing about him, apart from what he tells me.'

'Do you doubt what he tells you?'

'No . . . well, maybe, yes. I've always chosen not to be too attached to the truth.'

'And so this child is now coming to see you rather than your mother?'

'Yes, you could say that.'

'Well, he's made his choice,' Sayaka smiled. 'He's chosen you. It sounds like a wonderful thing to me.'

'I think he's lonely. He has problems at home.'

'We're all lonely. And we all have – or have had – problems at home. But we're not all capable of trust; trust is a precious thing.'

They continued talking quietly. Every so often, a train passed through the silence and birds took flight to patrol the sky, their shrieks fading into the distance. The train slipped into the side of the mountain, disappearing.

'What do you do together?'

'Nothing special,' Shūichi answered. Kenta did his homework; they leafed through the animal encyclopaedia together – animals were his great passion; he looked at his own books and took notes; they ate cakes and pancakes. Kenta was an obedient boy, but probably only because it wasn't often that somebody told him what to do.

'There are certain things you only do if someone tells you not to.'

Sayaka got up to go to the bathroom, turned around, and put a scarf around her shoulders.

They looked up and it was almost midnight.

As the silence descended, they realised they were alone. The other customers had all left a while ago; just the silhouette of the owner remained, tidying plates and knives.

The trust that Shūichi thought was like a bow and arrow

The city became quieter and quieter until it was silent.

The last train came in and left again as the night settled. Anyone wandering the streets of Kamakura now needed a good reason.

Sayaka and Shūichi crossed Wakamiya-ōji – the long, straight main road that led from Tsurugaoka Hachimangū temple to the sea.

'I'll walk you home,' Shūichi said, and Sayaka said she needed to get to her bike.

'Where is it?'

'On the seafront. I left it there because I felt like walking today.'

'Do you feel like walking a lot?'

'Yes, I always feel better when I'm moving my legs.'

The crowns of the cherry trees, distributed along

the sides of the road with military regularity, swayed vigorously while the stone lanterns hung still.

'You prepared my mother for her funeral,' said Shūichi. 'I remember now.'

Sayaka smiled. 'She was a beautiful woman, elegant. She looked after herself well. That's something you notice.'

'Is that not always the case?'

'No. It's nice when people look after themselves right up until the end.'

Trust is a drawn bow. Like the fear of William Tell, who put the apple on his son's head and fired the arrow knowing that, if his aim was misjudged, he had a second arrow hidden in his jacket ready to plunge into his own chest.

'The myth says that the second arrow was for the tyrant, but I believe it was for himself, to avoid surviving his son.'

They walked up the middle of the road, where the wind and the shadows of the elms met. The air, full of the sea, whipped across their faces.

'There's a video taken at a performance in 1980 by Marina Abramović and Ulay, her partner at the time. She is holding a huge bow and he is holding the arrow and the taut bowstring, pointed at her heart. Their heartbeats are amplified by microphones attached to their chests, translating their tension into sound. It lasts four minutes and twenty seconds, but it feels like an eternity.'

Shūichi took his phone out and stopped for a moment to show Sayaka an image of this woman and man in the middle of what looked like a ritual of love.

Seen from above, on the ruler-straight line of Wakamiya-ōji, Sayaka and Shūichi were a tiny luminous dot in the darkness.

'Amazing,' whispered Sayaka.

'I studied it for a book that I never finished. I wanted to use it to say that love is never alone. Fear is always right beside it.'

'If Ulay had been distracted and let go, the arrow would have pierced Marina's heart.'

'Love is precisely that risk.'

'Anyway, you've told me this story before.'

'I have?' Shūichi stopped, surprised.

'When you told me you had nothing to give me. "I have nothing to give you," you said.'

'I'm sorry.'

'You don't need to be sorry. It took me by surprise; it was as though you were reacting to something that hadn't even crossed my mind. I've always been a bit slow to catch on.'

'I was recently separated.'

'You saw danger everywhere,' Sayaka smiled.

'You're probably right.'

Sayaka had washed and dressed his mother's body and made up her face sweetly in preparation for the funeral a couple of months before. Shūichi, who had long been absent from himself, returned to that Thursday, to the precise moment that everything was happening, all thanks to Sayaka, to that slender woman he didn't yet know, who would slip discreetly from his memory when the ceremony ended.

There had been a moment of total intimacy: Sayaka helped him rub his mother's arms, legs and face with cinnamon-, rosemary- and violet-scented compresses, bathing her in the herbs and flowers she had loved most in life; she accompanied his fingers over his mother's small, white-haired head and whispered that, if he wanted, he could stay while she made up her face.

He watched the young woman's gentle hands, hands his mother didn't know and that were touching her for the first and last time, then let his gaze slip from his mother's body over Sayaka's smooth outline, her luminous, buttery skin; he felt confused.

Shūichi had mixed up the emotions of saying goodbye to his mother with the hazy memory of this woman and the voice that calmly explained the steps so that nothing would come as a surprise. Everything was wrapped up, the ceremony finished, and he went home.

Then there was an extraordinary coincidence that led, just one week later, to them sitting side by side on the train from Yokohama to Kamakura and, by an even more unlikely twist of fate, they had both felt like talking; they who usually avoided mixing with other people. Shūichi had just made the decision to move back to Kamakura, to clear out and renovate his childhood home.

And yet, from one meeting to the next, Shūichi had forgotten her, as if Sayaka had been the kind of person used to stepping aside to highlight a background or another person. She unravelled with time.

Each coincidence, though, seemed to immediately bring forth another.

As if just by knowing someone meant that from then on you would see them everywhere, Sayaka and Shūichi started meeting between supermarket shelves, queueing at the bank, outside the karaoke shop where she practised violin and he hid from the world when he needed to clear his head.

And so, for two months, Shūichi met her, then forgot her; met her, then forgot her.

It was the insistence of the coincidence that kept placing her in front of him that had pushed Shūichi, the evening they met twice — first at a red light and later in a pub — to say to Sayaka: 'I have nothing to give you.'

The trust that Kenta thought
was a word

For Kenta, trust was to do with words, and his mother never kept her word.

She made promises freely, got times wrong, went to pick him up an hour early despite having said he could play out until the sun set ('I was tired,' she'd explain, but what about her word? Where was her word?). His mother should have used the conditional, but she used the future; she did it so lightly. She felt obliged to always be right.

This was the problem with adults: they weren't sincere; they needed to tell lies. Because no one can always be right. And anyone who's fixated on being right needs to lie.

But Kenta believed her a little bit every time, not for lack of experience, but the desire to trust.

That was how his mother talked about dinners out, visiting his grandparents in Ōita, a trip to Luna

Park with his dad. Always next time, later, tomorrow, once spring arrives, when work calms down, when you're better, when I'm better, when everything's going better.

She was thoroughly convinced she was right, and that conviction drove Kenta mad. He wanted to be mistaken: he hoped, every time, that this time she was right.

That night, Shūichi looked at the clear outline of the mountain, its back curving under the lashes of the wind.

As a child, he and his mother had watched the mountain a thousand times as she got up on her feet, held her hunchback like an old lady and stretched out; they'd watched the houses and trees tumble down like crumbs from a beard.

Imagining was the game they liked best. One time, as his mother was cooking dinner in the kitchen, she had asked him to draw the things that they and nobody else had seen.

Now, tackling the steep slope of the road to the house and passing the cemetery on his right, Shūichi thought. He wondered what was different about his mother when she was not his mother, and why his mind had worked so hard to forget Sayaka.

He evaluated, for a matter of milliseconds, the option of letting go. He feared the kind of love that draws a circle and puts one person inside it. Shūichi knew one person was never enough to keep you alive; you needed many.

How was it possible that he still had this fear? He knew he was safe because he didn't have breath to be taken away or heartbeats to be skipped. He was sure that light had gone out a long time ago.

So he waited for morning, knowing that work – the jungle on the island where his book's protagonist had been washed up; the white, the green and the orange blended in his panels – would clear up the nostalgia and uncertainty. And in the afternoon Kenta would come with his big rucksack, exaggerated enthusiasm for stick insects and flying deer, and the monstruous *kanji* that came to life in his notebooks.

But night was still not drawing back, the darkness hung heavily.

A few hundred metres away, Kenta tossed and turned in his bed. His dreams muddled together things that had happened in real life with things he had wished would happen but hadn't. He woke suddenly with the taste of the sea in his mouth. He had jumped in and was drowning.

He would never tell Shūichi; he would never tell anyone.

What Kenta and Shūichi knew but wouldn't have been able to say

Adults can't console children because their worlds are too far apart. Children are content with love, and they know it's all that adults can give them.

Children can't console adults because adults don't give children that power. Adults console themselves by telling themselves that at least they have the ability to console children, but it's an illusion.

Shūichi unbuttoned his shirt.

With each button, the gap over his chest widened. Rather than a depression in the flesh, his mother noted after the surgery, the cut had left an elevation.

'It looks like a trench,' she had said, and he understood that in her mind that word defined the earth piled above the ground, not the hole that had been dug out. Shūichi had pulled his T-shirt back down, laughed and commented that she looked like she'd caught the sun.

She had just come home from a short trip. It was more, she said, like an extended prayer: she had thought of him the whole time. She had gone away while Shūichi's heart was being operated on because that was what her son wished. So she took the bus to the airport, then boarded a plane, then travelled a long way to a tiny hotel that looked out on the same sunset, moored boats, and an enormous ship that ploughed through tiny waves. Her journey was full of encounters between big and small and she often privately placed her palm over her chest, like she used to when Shūichi was young. She was convinced this was their secret language.

Trench. The word came to mind every time Shūichi thought every time he had a shower, unbuttoned his shirt or pulled a jumper over his head. He would bring his fingers to his chest, he too speaking their secret language. The thought lasted the time it took to say 'trench', and then he'd forget.

'Sit down.'

Shūichi obeyed and sat still in the seat, his eyes wide in waiting.

The cardiologist moved closer, placed the circle of metal on his chest and leaned in to listen. They were motionless, until the man closed the silence with a calm smile.

'All OK. Come again in six months.'

Doctor Fujita had been following the irregular beat of Shūichi's heart for more than a decade and being more or less the same age – and having met at the age of most intense transformation – had led them to talk about other things and to update one another on their lives. The register of their speech, however, remained formal.

'Thank you, Doctor,' Shūichi responded. He got up, gathered his clothes and repeated his actions in reverse: first the shirt, then the buttons from the bottom up.

'How are you? What are you writing at the moment? My daughter absolutely loved your book about the nightmare-eaters, the *Baku*, you know? She asked for a *Baku* for her birthday, but we didn't know where to get one,' the man laughed.

'People have really enjoyed that book,' Shūichi commented, 'boys the most, though.'

'Hana gets involved in whatever her little brother is interested in. She likes to learn things so that then she can teach him. They're currently going through a nightmares phase: imagining a creature that eats nightmares for dinner is thrilling for them both.'

'How old are they now?'

'Hana's thirteen and Yūto's four.'

'And how are they doing?'

'Yūto still has the asthma he was born with, but nothing to worry too much about. Hana has developed a crush on one of her classmates. My wife is more worried about her than about Yūto,' he laughed again.

Doctor Fujita's wife wasn't smiling in the photo that hung next to the degree and specialisation certificates behind his desk. Observing that perfectly composed face, controlled joy enclosed within a composition that saw her next to her husband and two children – one on her lap, the other at her side – always reminded Shūichi of his father. 'What do they have to laugh about?' he would often say about people they passed on the street. He couldn't understand why people smiled without good reason. 'But,' Shūichi's mother would whisper to him, 'a smile is the result of a long journey. Our faces are the sum of all the time we have spent building and maintaining it. It's not such a simple thing.'

Shūichi had met Doctor Fujita's wife only once and she hadn't smiled then either. 'My name is Yui,' she had said at the door of this office: he'd entered, she'd left. She was a small woman with still, intense eyes. Months later, Shūichi would hear that same voice on the radio: she was an announcer on a Tōkyō station.

'I've always wondered whether parents who are doctors worry less than parents who do other jobs,' Shūichi said.

'No, I don't think so. We are used to putting other people's minds at ease, but we are the most anxious of everyone: we know how things usually go, but we also know all the ways they could go wrong. The lesson we learn at work – that things work better when you are rational – only applies to work. As soon as we leave the surgery, we become human and impatient again.'

'Shame,' Shūichi laughed.

'No superpowers here,' the man smiled, sitting back down at his desk. 'I see you've changed your address.'

'Yes, I've moved back to Kamakura.'

'We had my mother's funeral in Kamakura many years ago, I think I told you.'

'Yes, I remember,' Shūichi replied. For a moment, he wondered whether Sayaka might have taken care of her body too. How old was Sayaka? She looked so young; who knew if she was working when

Doctor Fujita's mother died.

'I heard your mother has passed too . . . I'm sorry.'

'That's right, I had to change our last appointment because of the funeral.'

'And how's your heart?'

'The other one, you mean?'

The cardiologist nodded.

'The other one is still there. It doesn't move,' said Shūichi as he got up. 'I'll make the next appointment now, then.'

'Yes, you can do it online. I think you might need to wait a couple of weeks, though, as the bookings open five months in advance.'

'Thank you, doctor, goodbye.'

Then, in the doorway, before the bow that closed what it had opened half an hour earlier, the man put out his hand and placed it on Shūichi's shoulder.

'It never stops moving, really . . . the heart.'

Doctor Fujita looked at Shūichi intensely. His pupils sparkled with all the things he knew.

Shūichi didn't withdraw from his grip. He breathed deeply.

'It might not move for the same people or the same reasons. But it moves even when it seems still.'

The answer to the question about whether Sayaka had taken care of Doctor Fujita's mother's body too

Yes.

Shūichi got off the train at Kamakura station.

He chose the west exit because on the right-hand side there was a kiosk selling panda-shaped filled waffles. He ordered twelve: half filled with chocolate, the other half with cream.

With the paper cone in his hand, he set off towards the underpass that connected the two sides of the station, looking over at the little square with the clock tower as he passed. Some children were playing in the middle; a group of mums standing in the corner by the gelato shop. Not one of them was eating.

For some reason, Shūichi's attention was drawn to the square: maybe it was the noise, maybe the swarming clump of children on the ground. He only realised why when he saw that the small boy in the middle was Kenta. He smiled, wondering whether something inside him had recognised his little friend.

LAURA IMAI MESSINA

Kenta was laughing, his whole face crumpled, but Shūichi could tell it was fake laughter. Some of his friends were holding him down, others tickling him, but their movements were violent and Kenta got elbowed. A pair of boys were running to gather up soil and leaves from the flower beds to rub into his hair, and his clothes were filthy.

Shūichi had never seen Kenta's mother, so didn't know if she was among the group of women chatting in front of the gelato shop. He hesitated, wondering what the least humiliating course of action would be: to pretend not to have seen him? But what if Kenta had already seen him? Wasn't there a risk that Kenta would think he was like all the other adults, who only cared about bigger things, things that involved him, perhaps, but on which he had no right to an opinion?

Over the weeks they had spent together, Shūichi had understood that Kenta felt alone, and not because his parents were absent. It was more because of the lack of recognition of him as a person: they saw a son, but they didn't see Kenta, the specific child who, out of all the possible children, he was. They always wanted him to be different, more sensible, more grown up; uppercase where he was still lower. And beside them, Kenta felt wrong.

Just as he was about to walk into the underpass, Shūichi stopped. He retraced his footsteps and shouted from afar: 'Kenta! Kenta!'

The boy turned his head and the others, surprised, looked up.

Shūichi pulled his shoulders back and assumed the hard look that had saved him so many questions during his long years of school. 'Let's go,' he ordered drily.

The cluster of mums turned to scrutinise him; one made a small bow that he returned out of convention.

Hurry up, he thought.

The boy, out of breath, got up, collected his rucksack from a bush, and ran towards him. He turned back for a moment to wave at his classmates, who, inspecting Shūichi with bewilderment, didn't wave back.

'What were you doing?'
'We were playing.'
'Hm.'

'I was just being mean.'

'And do you like being mean?'

Kenta shrugged his shoulders.

'You mustn't play with them if it humiliates you. You are allowed to play another role if you don't like that one.'

'I know.'

They headed down Komachi-dōri and Shūichi rubbed Kenta's head, full of dry crushed leaves and soil, with his sleeve. He patted his dusty back.

'Why did you defend me?' Kenta suddenly asked.

'I once read that you should always be on the side of the dead.'

'But I'm not dead.'

'I know.'

Shūichi offered Kenta some of his stuffed pandas and the boy devoured them with such enthusiasm that he ended up giving him the whole bag.

'Do your parents know you come to my house every afternoon?'

'Yes.'

'Really?'

'Yes, I told you.'

Kenta darkened. Not being believed the first time

made him suspect that this man wouldn't have believed him the second or third either. Shūichi saw that thought evolve on the boy's face and changed the subject.

'I found something in my mother's drawer that I'd like your help with.'

'A mystery?'

Shūichi laughed. 'Yes, a mystery. At least until we figure out what it is.'

When, walking up the road to the house, they saw the first few long wooden sticks in the Buddhist cemetery, Kenta moved closer to Shūichi. He was used to monsters, like all children are, but the cemetery terrified him. Kenta said nothing, just touched Shūichi's hand. The man sensed the boy's fear. He felt dizzy, but shook it off before it invaded his mind.

He breathed in deeply. Then, without waiting for Kenta to become desperate, he spotted his little hand out of the corner of his eye. He stretched out his fingers and held the boy's hand tightly inside his.

Without looking at one another, they continued up the road.

The conversation Shūichi had with a documentary-maker friend and what Shūichi meant when he said you should always be on the side of the dead

M: 'I am always amazed. Why do you think the elderly still lament the wrongs they were done in childhood, even after seventy or eighty years? And by wrongs, I don't just mean the war or a serious trauma, but a toy confiscated, an insult thrown by a classmate at kindergarten, or a beating doled out unfairly by a grandparent. Can it really be possible that they're still not over it? I mean, not only has the moment passed and nothing can be done, but the child they were has vanished. Vanished along with all the emotions that child experienced.'

S: 'Yes, the child they were is basically dead. But they remain forever on the side of that child.'

M: 'But so much time has passed . . .'

S: 'That doesn't change a thing. We remain forever on the side of the dead.'

Few things had happened in the preceding weeks. But they were all important.

One was opening the bottom drawer in his mother's bedside table.

Shūichi was looking for her passport to return it to the Kanagawa prefectural office. Of the whole house, his mother's room was the only one that remained locked, even throughout the weeks when Shūichi was furiously throwing everything away to free himself of her memory.

Going into the room, he was struck by the peculiar sensation you experience on realising you were once a child. He had left his heart behind all those years ago, and a part of it remained there.

His mother's bedroom was like a cave. On the walls were sheets of paper Shūichi had given her over the years: his most elementary sketches evolved into intricately detailed scenes; the characters' mouths and noses gradually shifted into place; the proportions that were all wrong at first were made almost too right, eventually relaxing into something that, with repetition, had become his style. In Shūichi's drawings, there were always windows, and the windows served as frames or portals, and every story took place within

105

these frames that opened and closed the house's communication with all that surrounded it. Shūichi was touched by the way that, between the drawings he'd done at the age of three and the whole strips he'd completed at almost forty, there was no hierarchy of importance. Everything had been important!

When he opened the bottom drawer of the bedside table, so low down he imagined it had been sealed for years, Shūichi was surprised by the cold air that wafted out. It must have been winter when it was last closed.

He didn't find her passport but lots of other bits and pieces: two CDs, some jewellery, a pair of earplugs and his mother's handwriting on a Post-it note that read: 'For Shūichi'.

The Post-it was stuck to a little box no bigger than an apricot.

He opened the apricot and there was a hazelnut.

He opened the hazelnut and found a seed.

Inside the seed was a tiny paper worm.

Shūichi unrolled it and his eyes stretched wide in amazement. Out of the cocoon came another, almost identical to the first. He read them one after the other. He didn't understand. He inverted the order.

He read them aloud in a whisper, hoping that, in the sound, whatever these papers were hiding would come out into the light.

Nothing. It meant nothing.

In one last attempt, he tried in English. Maybe it was a play on words?

Nothing.

What was written on the first tiny
piece of paper

42191

What was written on the second
tiny piece of paper

42192

The same afternoon that Shūichi rescued Kenta from his schoolmates in the square with the clock tower and held his hand walking up towards the Concubine's Tunnel, he showed the boy the pieces of paper.

'What does it mean?' the little boy asked, bewildered.

'I don't know, I was hoping you'd help me decipher them.'

'So it is a real mystery!' The child was excited.

'If we don't work it out, unfortunately it will remain a mystery,' Shūichi said.

'But mysteries are fun!' And to reassure him that he believed his own words, Kenta opened his school bag and pulled out a book entitled *The Mystery of Kanji*. He had borrowed it from the school library that morning.

'If they are made-up mysteries, yes, they're fun,

but if they're about your own life, they're just missing pieces.'

Shūichi got up and went into the kitchen to prepare their snack. Two little plates, two little forks, two glasses of chocolate milk.

Kenta, meanwhile, flicked through the book and read his favourite bits out loud.

Kenta was probably right, Shūichi thought as he unwrapped the strawberry cake and placed it carefully on the little plate. But mysteries were strewn all over his childhood: memories he wasn't sure were his; nice things that happened to other people which he confused as things that happened to him; other things that were taken away from him by his mother because they weren't happy enough.

'Do you want fizzy orange too?'

'Is there any apple juice?'

Shūichi thought about it while he looked in the fridge. For example, the trip to Nagano when he was ten, shredded memories that had been visiting him in his dreams recently: the snow three metres high that made every road into a bastion; the red-faced monkeys floating in the hot springs; the oyaki

110

dumplings that were so delicious he insisted on having them for breakfast, lunch and dinner. But in Nagano he also rode a horse and was maybe thrown off: he landed on his back and his mother screamed — he physically remembered the sound. And if, as a child, Shūichi ever asked about Nagano, his mother would change the subject so determinedly that at a certain point he started to wonder if any of it was real: the compact walls of snow, the monkeys, the spring rolls filled with *adzuki* beans, the horse's tense body as it suddenly arched its back.

'Here you go,' he said, placing the glass full of yellow liquid down next to Kenta.

Shūichi arranged the little cake and the cups and sat down next to him, immersed in his own thoughts.

There were holes in Shūichi's past, like the game where you're shown some images for a few seconds, and then, skipping to different versions of the images with half of the things missing, you have to identify what's missing.

In certain moments, when Shūichi was sitting in the armchair and Kenta was tapping his pen against his notebook, the man raised his eyes and, in his head, asked: *What did she tell you about me? What did my mother tell you about my childhood?* Then he felt ridiculous and lowered his eyes again. But the questions remained. How much did that child know that he didn't? How much had his mother revealed to Kenta that he couldn't remember?

'Shall we read? Do you feel like it?' Kenta said in that moment, finishing off the strawberry cake.

Shūichi put down his fork and nodded.

For weeks, they had been studying the origins of ideogramss: how snow 雪 was a hand sweeping away the rain, how rain 雨 could also be found in cloud 雲, mist 霞, fog 霧 and quake 震.

'Why?' asked Kenta. 'What do earthquakes have in common with storms?'

They also discovered that love 愛 meant to look behind you and hesitate, that husband 夫 had a pin stuck into his hair, and that evening 夜 kept the moon under its roof.

Shūichi drew them, Kenta listened enraptured, and together they came up with absurd relationships between the original signs and the meanings attributed to them over time. They often seemed like errors. How else could the immense distance between a word's origin and what people used it for be justified?

That was when Shūichi remembered an afternoon thirty years ago when his mother explained the meaning of the ideogram for 'lie' 嘘 and how it was born out of an abandoned village whose buildings had all fallen into ruin. It seemed even more wonderful than when he had first heard it, perhaps because in telling the boy the story of something that now tormented him, he was substituting the vagueness of ceaselessly confirmed and denied memories with the concreteness of houses and cemeteries perched on a mountainside.

Seeing it practically, replacing the fog, felt like a gift.

Why, according to Shūichi, lies were places in ruin, and what, according to Kenta, happened to them

Shūichi had read it in the dictionary of Shirakawa, a scholar his mother venerated.

She didn't venerate him so much because of the anthropological rigour she described repeatedly as being 'of a fineness never before surpassed', but because of the enthusiasm and curiosity with which he told the stories of the *kanji*, the way he brought them to life.

'See, Shūichi, lies are places in ruin,' and with her chalk she'd draw the strokes, one at a time. 'The *kanji* for lie is this, look.'

嘘

'It is a mouth 口 and a hill 丘, on which once upon a time sat an ancient city. It was full of sacred places, buildings of varying importance, and it was home to a cemetery.'

'A cemetery?' Shūichi repeated.

'Yes, that's important. Until somebody dies and somebody is born, a city has no history.'

The child looked uncertain.

'Then, one day, the city was abandoned.'

'Why, Mum?' he interrupted.

'Who knows why . . . but it was eroded by the weather and fell into ruin. And what remained there was just rubble, relics and disused buildings. That's how, putting the ideogram for this story alongside the one for mouth, the *kanji* for lie 嘘 was born.'

Mrs Ōno wrote it again on the board, first fast, then slow.

$$口 + 虚 = 嘘$$

'See, that's what lies are in our language: useless things, things with no substance. Do you understand, Shūichi?'

'So lies have no purpose?' he asked, bringing his pencil to his lips. He always chewed the wood as soon as his mother turned around.

'Hmm . . . I don't completely agree with that. I think, depending on the situation, lies can be very useful.'

'For what?'

The woman looked at him intensely and, after thirty years, Shūichi could still feel the moment of her response, the really intense way his mother settled inside him when she wanted to be completely honest but feared hurting him.

'What are lies good for, Mum?'

'They're good for improving our memories.'

Decades later, Shūichi was sitting next to Kenta in the living room and explaining the same thing to him, using the same words.

'Look what happens to places when humans abandon them,' he said, showing the child a photo. It was of a bathroom: four little washbasins along the wall, flaking paint, a crumbling ceiling and a tree coming up through the floor. The branches of the plant, indifferent to its surroundings, reached towards the light that had broken through the glass and invaded the space.

'But did it used to be a school?'

116

'Yes, a school bathroom. But not any more.'

Shūichi observed the child's face. It was so serious that he thought he would never be able to distinguish whether he was happy or sad.

'So now,' said Kenta in a calm voice, 'it can become a school for wild animals. It can be a school for foxes and *tanuki*!'

Part Two
きゅん kyun

Everything [pain] touches is promoted to the rank of a memory; it leaves traces in the recollection which pleasure merely grazes.

—EMIL CIORAN, TR. RICHARD HOWARD

Teshima, Summer
豊島　夏

ASTRONG WIND BLOWS ON THE island of
Teshima.

It is summer and the cicada's song is deafening.

A white bus runs along narrow streets, climbs up
hills, slips into woods, and emerges suddenly in front
of the sea. On board, an old woman holds a piece
of paper in her hand. She looks at it pensively; she
fears it will not be useful. She has no confidence
when it comes to numbers, or the Western alphabet.
She tries nonetheless to make them make sense: she
puts on her glasses and reads aloud.

'Now, here it says that the coordinates are 34° 48'N 134° 10'E, coastline 19.8 kilometres, area 14.4 kilometres squared, elevation 340 metres.'

'Elev—?'

'I think it means height,' she responds, hesitantly. 'The address is 2801-1 Karato Teshima, Tonoshō-chō, Shōzu-gun, Kagawa 7614662.'

'Have you put it into the map on your phone?' the young boy next to her asks. They've been travelling together for twenty-four hours and he's tired now.

'No, I don't really know how to use it.'

The boy looks concerned.

'Don't worry, we'll get there,' the woman smiles. 'It's sort of like a pilgrimage: I read that you have to get a bit lost in order to find it.'

The bus bumps along the road, making them bounce in their seats. It's tiny compared to the ones they're used to taking in the city. When they boarded, they chose the seats at the back so they could see more of the view.

The boy grumbles. He would've preferred to stay in Takamatsu or Naoshima. There's nothing in Teshima, just museums, rice fields and water. But the

main reason for his bad mood is that he left the electronic encyclopaedia his father gave him in the hotel.

The recorded female voice announces the next
stop as the bus continues to weave through windy
streets, run along tarmacked roads, and slow down
on a dirt track. There isn't any air-con, or if there
is it must have been switched off because the windows
are all open and a warm, perfumed breeze wafts in,
reminding the passengers of their proximity to the
sea.

The bus stops often and the boy sighs. 'Why is it
so uncomfortable?'

'Discomfort is good for your memory,' the lady
responds happily. Her face is full of wrinkles, but she
must have once been quite beautiful. She wouldn't
know what to do with beauty now. 'Look out the
window and think of the extraordinary place we're
going to visit.'

After a sweeping curve, the rice fields open up.
They look like a blanket of matcha chocolate. 'I'm
hungry,' he announces, but the old lady doesn't
respond, just looks at him with a kind smile.

'Isn't your heart beating fast?'

They are on this small bus, thousands of miles from home, because of a magazine she was flicking through two weeks ago at the hairdresser's. An artist from a country she didn't know, who spoke a language she didn't know, was writing about the Heartbeat Archive in Teshima. She knows nothing about contemporary art, but the artist's words moved her deeply.

She had planned a whole other holiday with the boy, maximum one train journey from home and a hotel full of amenities and activities, but when she read that in the south-west of Japan there was a library full of not books, but heartbeats, she felt fate had come looking for her.

The boy was not convinced: 'Isn't it too far away?' he protested at first, but she, who usually gave in, didn't this time.

'Let's go to Teshima!' she insisted. 'Everything is telling us that this is the perfect place for our trip!'

The same day that the old lady read the interview, she went to a bookshop and bought the magazine. It was heavy, so she cut out the bit she was interested in. In the evening, she put on her reading glasses and folded the paper up until it just showed the paragraph that had convinced her. She put it in her handbag and it had stayed there ever since.

She read it many times before the trip, including to the boy, who remained in silence – not because he understood deep down what it meant, but because the way she placed her voice carefully on the words revealed how much it meant to her.

This is a difficult year. He's nervous because he feels he needs to grow up quickly: his mother, his father, the exams at school, but he loves her. He loves her so much that he says nothing, not even when she takes the cut-out from her bag for the hundredth time and, despite the bends and bumpiness of the bus, she reads aloud: *'It's a place that is not easy to reach. It's a quiet and beautiful island far from Tōkyō, far from any big city in the world. This is a journey you take to listen to someone's heart.* Isn't it wonderful?'

The boy nods.

'Isn't it incredible? Suddenly all of humanity feels near!'

The bus slows down and the recorded voice announces: 'Teshima Art Museum: push the button if you would like to disembark here.' Two girls of around twenty press it and the bell rings.

125

'The next stop is us,' says the lady and the boy nods his head.

The sea on the horizon is dotted with peanut-sized boats. The boy stares at a hump that bulges out of the water; one of the dozens of islands that float around Teshima. He saw them from the plane the day before when they were coming in to land at Takamatsu as the sun was setting, and the sea looked like a table scattered with golden breadcrumbs.

Out of the window, a dragonfly hovers over the bus stop sign. The woman smiles proudly: she never thought, at her age, she'd be capable of such a journey.

She folds the magazine clipping up and puts it back in her handbag.

This island is roughly the shape of a heart.

Seen from the nearby island of Shōdoshima, Teshima looks like the back of a fist, closed protectively around something precious. That's where the first part of its name comes from: 'Te' meaning 'hand'.

As they walk between two rice paddies and arrive at the beach behind which the Archive sits, the woman repeats the artist's words like a prayer.

126

She remembers the photo of the artist in the magazine with his shaved head, strong body and kind eyes. She was won over by the calmness with which he affirmed immense things; with which he accepted them.

The air already resounds with the sound of somebody's heart.

She sits down on a bench. 'Sorry, I just need to rest for a moment.'

The boy is happy again, he's not bothered by having to wait. All around him, swarms of solitary dragonflies float up in flight, meeting in the air. They rise and fall around the tiny cluster of fishermen's houses that make this place a village. The boy loves watching them, he's never seen so many in his life. They're blue, yellow and pink. His father taught him that if you stick a finger out and wait, one might eventually land on it.

'Look!' he exclaims when a dragonfly finally pauses on his pointed index finger.

The old woman smiles. The boy reminds her of her son in his happiest moments. She closes her eyes and breathes in the sea air.

What matters most, the artist wrote, *is to preserve our*

memory, because people come back to life only in the memory of others.

When she feels old and useless, when she thinks she has been imprudent to bring the boy all this way from home, when the boy complains that he's bored and tired, the woman rubs him on the head and responds, with a certainty she has rarely had, that this very idea is what makes the trip worth it.

'Preserving our memory . . . because people come back to life only in the memory of others.'

chapter
one

IN THE WEEKS THAT FOLLOWED, Shūichi's work
shifted into reverse.

With Kenta's help, he reopened all the boxes he
had packaged up. Kenta couldn't believe his luck
at being able to pick up his old habit of going to
that house on his way home from school, doing his
homework at the living-room table, eating a snack
prepared for him and asking for help whenever he
needed it.

Shūichi salvaged the dishes, the schoolbooks and
the ornaments from the garage. In the mornings, he

worked on his book with great focus so that his afternoons would be free.

'No, you're wrong! That goes there, on the book-case, not on the wardrobe!'

Kenta remembered everything off by heart; he corrected Shūichi and made him reposition the objects following the path of his pointed finger. The boy didn't stop reprimanding him, but he began to sound more like a song than anything else.

Faced with certain objects and toys, they were both silenced, and Shūichi kept wondering at what point the boy had learned about him.

When Shūichi asked him why on earth he took the watering can and the frying pan, and what he'd done with all his mother's comic books and trinkets, Kenta told him he'd hidden them in his room, under the bed, in his toy basket, in his drawers. He planned to buy their house in the future and put all the things back in their places. He didn't realise how absurd the idea sounded when it was said out loud.

They went down to Kenta's house. Shūichi waited for him outside with a big cart, like the ones you carry baggage, or children, in. It took Kenta four trips to bring everything out.

While waiting in front of the house, Shūichi looked at the objects pressed against the windows, the curtain squashed by the weight of something, the neglected garden, the enormous car occupying the parking space.

Shūichi hated houses full of things, which is why he drew only windows in his books. It seemed to him a contradiction: people bought beautiful houses, spent millions of yen so that the windows would face south, the wood would be cedar and the ceramics in the cabinet would be from the most exclusive potters, but then accumulated so much stuff that you could no longer see any of it; even the light had to make space for itself like water seeping between the furniture and clutter.

Listening to Kenta, Shūichi had intuited how difficult his family situation was, however common. His parents were at the stage where they needed to decide whether to persevere, to wait, or to go their separate ways. They were together but already living completely distinct lives.

The house confirmed this impression.

When they were finished, Shūichi's house looked just like it did before, just cleaner and tidier.

The man smiled at all the effort he'd gone to to expel his mother from the house and how, in just a few weeks, and thanks to the intervention of this mysterious boy, she might as well have turned up on the doorstep with her seraphic calm and a giant suitcase, back from a trip she'd rather enjoyed.

'Are these your books?' Kenta asked. 'The ones you wrote?'

He was holding out a large book with a walnut shell on its cover.

'Did you win a big prize for this one?'

'How do you know?'

'Mrs Ōno told me about it.'

Of course, thought Shūichi.

'Why did you throw it out?'

'I don't know. It's from the past. I prefer to think about the future when I work.'

He had written that book at the age of twenty-three. It was inspired by the memory of his grandfather, a man who was already old when he was born. A quiet and gloomy man, he didn't ask questions and rarely spoke to anyone. Shūichi's mother had explained that he had gone through the Second World War and only part of him had come back.

132

Before he left, she said, he was a cheerful man, full of stories. But Shūichi never managed to imagine him differently. Only as an adult, watching a documentary about war veterans, had Shūichi finally understood: it wasn't just bodies that were lost, but souls. He dedicated the book to his grandfather and his mother: to pay homage to the man who disappeared, and to compensate, in a way, his mother, the daughter of the man who she loved equally before and after. The book was his final piece for his degree.

'But what do walnuts have to do with your grandpa?' Kenta asked.

Shūichi had searched long and hard for an image capable of representing his absent yet still present grandfather who he had visited regularly until he was nine years old. One morning, boarding a train full of commuters heading to Tōkyō, he saw a man with a bag on his lap, sitting on a bench on the platform, motionless while the world swirled around him. From then on, Shūichi started to notice people, young and old, dressed in expensive suits or cheap dresses, who, at random times of random days, were motionless. They seemed like shelled walnuts waiting for everything around them to stop. There were no kernels, just the hulls and the shells.

It was received as a work that could explain the ordeal of those suffering from post-traumatic disorders in a light-hearted way, and it brought Shūichi success.

'Have you ever cracked a walnut?'

'I've only ever seen them already open.'

Shūichi got up, took a nutcracker out of the drawer and found a nut in the cupboard.

'I don't really like walnuts . . .'

'You don't have to eat it,' Shūichi smiled. 'Wedge the nut in here, then squeeze the handles . . . Harder, that's it.'

They picked the nut clean with their fingers and Kenta touched the lignified septum, the shell, the kernel.

'It's like a mummy.'

'Huh?'

Shūichi looked into Kenta's eyes, the bright black-ness of his pupils.

'They took the guts out of the mummies in Egypt, didn't they?'

'Actually, they didn't take out all of their insides,' Shūichi specified. 'They left in their hearts.'

134

'Their hearts?'

'They believed that the dead needed their hearts in order to get to the netherworld.'

'So the heart was like a kind of compass?'

'Yes, I suppose so . . .'

Shūichi turned to the window and forced himself to remain composed. He had been asked that question, in exactly the same tone of voice, many years earlier. Back then, it was the middle of the night, now it was daytime.

'Mrs Ōno told me that your heart is different from other people's.'

'It's nothing serious.'

'What is your sickness called?'

'It's not actually a sickness, and the name is difficult.'

'How so?'

'*Paroxysmal supraventricular tachycardia*,' he pronounced.

Kenta opened his eyes wide.

'I told you it was difficult.'

'Mrs Ōno told me that you couldn't do heavy exercise or feel strong emotions.'

'My mother always made it into something bigger

135

than it was,' Shūichi concluded. 'Come on now, finish your homework, I need to get on with my reading.'

Kenta returned to the table and picked up his pencil. Shūichi settled in the armchair with a pile of books, magazines and photocopied newspaper articles about desert islands and shipwrecks.

Around ten minutes passed before Kenta interrupted the silence again.

Shūichi tensed his jaw: he desperately needed to work out what the little protagonist of his book would see. He had just arrived on the island; what kind of vegetation was there? And was the beach stony or sandy? Was the sand dark or white? He had to go to Tōkyō the following Monday to hand in his first pages to the editor, and the big moving of objects, the dense conversations with Kenta and the unforeseen adaptation to his daily routine had put him way behind schedule.

He was about to ask the boy to hold it in and wait for their break, when Kenta came out with a sentence that meant Shūichi could no longer say nothing.

'Mrs Ōno told me about when you went down the hill on your bike . . .'

Shūichi stopped. He was holding the map of an uninhabited island in the Indian Ocean. He was speechless, the paper in mid-air.

'The scar you have on your arm is from the twenty stitches you had, right?' Kenta continued. 'It must have been exciting going down there. I can't even imagine how fast you must have gone with ice on that road!' He pointed towards the road outside the square window.

'Ice?' Shūichi asked, trying not to reveal his surprise.

'It had snowed the day before and the road was icy, wasn't it? Mrs Ōno said you loved the snow so much you'd even gone out and eaten it the day before,' he exclaimed, laughing.

It was true, it was cold that day. He had forgotten.

'Staying in bed for weeks must have been *sooo* boring. But that's what made you start drawing, right?' the boy added. 'I would love to be able to stay in bed reading manga all day for a month.'

Like the mouths of carps that greedily break the surface of the water as soon as the sound of footsteps comes near, the memory emerged in Shūichi's mind of his parents' bed, the side onto which his mother

137

transferred his weight every morning, the room big and full of light, his books, the bookstand, his broken left arm, the box of pencils, his mobile right hand. It all came back to him.

'Many artists started their careers because of an accident. Charles Dickens, Frida Kahlo . . . if not immobilised in bed, it's rare for someone to choose to do something as boring as writing or drawing,' Shūichi changed the subject. 'People prefer to live, and in general that's the best choice.'

'When you say it like that, it makes me want to break my leg!'

They both laughed.

'Now study.'

For the next hour, you could hear a pin drop, but Shūichi could no longer concentrate on his reading.

Night filled the street and Kenta was scared. Shūichi was also scared, but it was a different kind of fear.

The cemetery by the side of the curve in the road seemed bigger, with thousands of wooden sticks, and Kenta imagined an army of the dead, marching towards him armed with questions, like messengers from a past world, suddenly launched, despite themselves, into the future. He didn't imagine them as angry, more bewildered. But he couldn't help them; he knew nothing.

When he was alone, to avoid having to pass the cemetery, Kenta walked around the mountain, climbing the hill on the opposite side of the Concubine's Tunnel. Shūichi sensed the boy's fear so, after sunset, he'd accompany him to the bottom of the road and then go back up.

But that evening Shūichi didn't go home.

The conversation with Kenta, the long-denied memory of the accident re-entering his life in such an unexpected way, even the fact of feigning unsurprise in front of the boy, had drained him. He was exhausted. Perhaps I'll go for a walk, he thought, and get something to eat in town.

In the fish-and-sake restaurant in an alleyway off Komachi-dori, sitting alone at a little table at the back, ruminating on how it was possible that memories could all come to the surface in one go, it happened: from the cold of the morning when he was five, to the sensation of the snow on his teeth; the immaculate silence of his mother at the hospital and those wonderful days of convalescence; then the darkness of the incident at the neighbour's house, when her two-year-old son leaned over to look into the top-loading washing machine, full of water, and drowned, the sirens; his father slamming the door and saying he was worthless; peeing himself at school and leaving without permission to avoid humiliation in front of his classmates.

They were all unhappy memories, memories that, thanks to his mother's persistence in denying all that was sad, he had never been sure were real; yet now they felt touching and precious, even more precious than the fantastic trips his mother talked about, which she added new and different details to every time they talked. More than his winnings at the Luna Park shooting games; more than the infinite rotation of the carousel at Yokohama, which, one afternoon in August, by magic, just didn't stop; and even more than his father's infinite cuddles, a memory of which he really struggled to muster.

Tears pricked Shūichi's eyes, and the more he thought about the terrible things that had happened in his life, the more precious they seemed.

He smiled. So it was true, memories could sit

140

quietly for years and then, all at once and all together, rise up, like bamboo plants split from the same mother: wherever they have been planted in the world, they all flower on the same day.

That was the evening Shūichi met Sayaka.

doki doki

'When do things become our own?'

'Completely?'

'Yeah, our own, forever.'

'Like what?'

'I don't know . . . like a house?'

'If you move, then maybe it's not yours forever. Parents should stay, though, if they don't die first. Parents never leave us.'

'What about friends?'

'But why do you want to know?'

'Because.'

The older boy and the younger boy played for a long time; one brought a big ball, the other brought swimming trunks. They went down to the beach and spent three hours by the sea. After they were done throwing and catching the ball, they built a complex marble track. Then they caught crabs, but the younger boy accidentally trod on one of them and then they stopped completely, terrified of accidentally killing them. The older boy found a starfish which had almost dried out and was missing an arm or a leg. They squatted down looking at it for a long time, dazzled by its beauty, telling each other everything they knew about starfish.

'Starfish completely regrow themselves.'

'I read in my encyclopaedia that they eat shellfish, sea urchins and molluscs. There was a photo where one had eaten a whole crab!'

'They can die after just a few seconds out of the water. You should never take them out to look at them!'

Then, before they went home, they put it back in the sea because, even if it had been dead for a while, the older boy's grandma said you shouldn't mix up the kingdoms. Things in the sea should stay in the sea, and things on the land should stay on the land; including things like plastic and paper. He did sometimes collect shells though, as they were small enough to hide in his pocket.

The sun was setting when they left the beach. They were so tired, they walked in silence.

That was when the younger boy asked the older boy his question, the only question that he really wanted an answer to.

'And you, will you be my friend forever?'

Kenta often dreamed out loud.

Announcing that he was an explorer about to go deep into a jungle, traipsing down the long, raised walkway that ran down the middle of the main road in Kamakura became an adventure.

The sharp branches of the six-year-old cherry trees that stood on either side of the road in perfect symmetry transmuted into a web of vines and rain-forest vegetation among which stalked not crows and squirrels, but toucans, Bengal foxes and royal cobras.

It wasn't a lie: for Kenta, whatever was said aloud immediately came into being.

Shūichi had intuited it watching him from the armchair in the afternoons. When a conversation didn't interest him, Kenta's mind started to wander; he would whisper scenes from an imaginary battle and every so often make shooting sounds and do karate moves.

145

Shūichi understood that Kenta's wild imagination wasn't just daydreaming but that it permeated his whole life when, one afternoon at the end of winter, he found him with his eyes closed, standing in the middle of the Wakamiya-ōji main road.

The boy was getting ready to cross the dip, the most crowded part of the stone walkway. He searched in his blindness for correspondences between steps, the length and speed at which people decided on their direction, and then, without warning, he charged straight across in the vain hope of avoiding collision. People mostly moved out of his way, or Kenta would bump into an arm or a leg. Holding onto his spirit, he continued.

Then something happened that Shūichi hadn't expected. Kenta ran into a woman's stomach and the woman, rather than moving out of his way, extended her arms. She laughed, and the boy laughed too, opening his eyes wide in surprise.

She was Sayaka, he was Kenta. The two newest things in his life.

Shūichi looked up. Petals fell from the sky, declaring the start of spring.

After the evening they met at the fish–and–sake restaurant next to the station, Shūichi knew he wouldn't
forget her again.

This time, the woman's features were firm in his
mind, as was the sense that she did not want anything
from him.

Shūichi didn't look for her, nor she him. But they
were both convinced that there was something there,
the nature of which neither could articulate.

Shūichi remembered her sitting on the other side
of the table, with her strange mannerism of raising
her index finger before speaking. Like a child, she
made sure she had his attention before saying what
she had to say.

Strangely, in the weeks after that evening, Shūichi
did not meet her on the streets of Kamakura. Yet
he knew, in that widening of time, that Sayaka was
completing the gesture: the taut bow between her
stomach and his chest, him still, her contemplating
the possibility of letting go and piercing his heart.

'Kenta, this is Sayaka,' Shūichi laughed, his palm
opened out to the woman Kenta had run into.

The child, looking up, immediately knew that

147

his friend and this woman were tangled up in some way.

'This is Kenta, I think I told you about him.' It was the first time Shūichi had spoken to Sayaka using an informal register.

'Yes, I remember. Nice to meet you Kenta, I'm Sayaka.'

'What a funny way to meet.'

'I was on my way home from a consultation with my brother in Yukinoshita.'

'I'm hungry, I want crêpes!' the boy interrupted. 'I *reeeeeally* want crêpes!'

'Well, if it's that bad, we should get crêpes, shouldn't we?' said Sayaka.

She suggested the little stand in Onari-dori, the sister shop of the more popular one in the street-food market around the corner. 'The queue's half as long and it's just as good.'

As they crossed Wakamiya-ōji, slaloming around the tourists who filled the city, Sayaka asked Shūichi: 'How's your work going, the book about the shipwreck?'

'On Saturday I'm going to Tōkyō to hand in the first block of panels.'

'Wow, it's going well then.'

Kenta ordered a strawberry crêpe and Shūichi was once again taken aback by the simplicity of the boy's taste in food. Since they had met, Kenta had ordered ice cream, crêpes, sundaes, and cakes, but always strawberry flavour.

Sayaka got a salted caramel one and Shūichi added whipped cream and toasted almonds to it.

'Can I come with you on Saturday?' Kenta asked. 'To Tōkyō?'

'Sorry, don't you have school?'

'There's no school on Saturdays.'

'And you're not going out with your parents?'

'They're both working.'

Shūichi was about to ask another question when Kenta turned to Sayaka: 'How about you?'

'What about me?'

'Are you free on Saturday?'

Shūichi didn't understand what was going on.

'The day after tomorrow is *tomo-biki*, so yes.'

Kenta furrowed his eyebrows.

'My work is to do with funerals.'

'You work with dead people? Cool!'

Shūichi stood to one side and smiled.

149

'We never have funerals on *tomo-biki* days: it's supposed to be bad luck, did you know that?'

Kenta shook his head.

'If you write *tomo-biki*, you'll see that it has the *kanji* for "friend" and "pull" in it,' said Sayaka, showing him the characters on her phone. 'So it's kind of like the dead person risks pulling their friends into their grave with them.'

'It would be terrible! You go to your friend's funeral and end up dead!'

'That's why we avoid holding funerals on those days.'

'Then we can go to Tōkyō together. We can visit the Pokémon exhibit in Shibuya! It's at the Bunkamura and Saturday is the last day it's open!'

Shūichi suddenly caught up with what Kenta was suggesting. 'The last day?'

'Yes!'

'But imagine the queues . . .'

'But then it's closing forever! Forever!'

The drama in Kenta's voice made Shūichi and Sayaka laugh.

'Please can we go!' Kenta begged. 'Come on! I could use it for a school project. My parents never take me anywhere, I'll finally have something cool to write about.'

Shūichi started laughing, first quietly, then louder. It was funny to witness Kenta's scheme. He had backed him into a corner and he knew that involving Sayaka was a strong move.

'OK, I'm in,' Shūichi said. 'You're very bad, though.' Then, turning to Sayaka, who was already nodding: 'Only if you want to, of course.'

'Yes, why not.'

'Meet at the station at nine?'

That afternoon, after waving goodbye to Sayaka in front of the crêpe shop, Kenta and Shūichi headed home. Kenta turned to Shūichi, breaking the silence.

'Do you like her?'

'What do you mean? In what way?'

'Do you like Sayaka-san? Are you in love with her?'

'Oh, come on.'

'You like her though . . .'

'I don't not like her. Why are you asking me these questions?'

'Hm,' Kenta mumbled, pensive. The reason he asked was actually to do with something Mrs Ōno

151

had told him once, and another thing that his mother had said to him more recently. Both were to do with being alone, but he didn't know how to explain them.

The evening was fresh, the air smelled of flowers and Shūichi wondered where the scent was coming from.

'If you like her, though, why don't you ask her out?'

'Because . . . I'm not happy enough.'

The boy raised his eyebrows and Shūichi was surprised by his own response.

'If you don't think you can improve a person's life, it's not fair to place yourself next to them.'

'So you're not happy?'

'I don't know. Maybe not happy enough to invite a woman out.'

They got to the bridge that crossed the Nameri river. Shūichi looked over the edge. The heads of peonies were beginning to fall, February was nearing its end. That was where the smell was coming from.

'But couldn't it be her who makes you happy?' Kenta restarted. 'Or maybe she's not looking for someone to make her happy; maybe she's just fine.'

Shūichi smiled but didn't reply.

'Anyway, it's not true.'

'What isn't?'

'It's not true that you can't make someone's life better. You make my life better, for example.'

Then, without waiting for a reaction, Kenta started running.

'See you tomorrow! I'll come round after school!' he shouted while running, almost fearing that he'd jinx it if he said those words again.

The upstairs windows of the small house were lit up; Kenta's parents must have come home recently. Shūichi waited for the boy to close the door behind him and then started the climb.

doki doki

'It's my birthday today.'

'I know. It's my birthday too.'

'Are you having a cake?'

'My grandma said she'll make me one with straw-berries and cream.'

'My mum's going to buy me one; we're going to choose it from the cake shop tonight.'

'Isn't it strange that our birthdays are on the same day?'

'A bit. Do you think it means something?'

'Like what?'

The younger boy was silent. All the love he felt needed facts, handholds in the real world. He was constantly looking for them. He would have liked to say then that the dates were the same because they were born to be friends, that nobody would ever separate them. Even imagining saying it made him

154

feel silly. He changed the subject.

'What job do you want to do when you're older?'

'You say first.'

'An aeroplane pilot. I want to fly.'

'You can fly without becoming a pilot. Like take a plane somewhere, or hire a helicopter . . .'

'But you have to pay. It costs loads to fly.'

'True . . .'

'And you?'

'My dad's job. Mum always says that he sees more things than other people do. Millions of things more than other people. Not because he has better eyesight than other people, but because he wants to see them.'

The younger boy didn't understand. 'You mean you want to see lots of things?'

'Lots of things in a small space. That way you don't have to go very far to be happy.'

The boy adored the things his older friend said, full of pauses and so many certainties it seemed like they came from a book. He wasn't sure about anything himself, and hearing his friend talk made him feel happy. Maybe he didn't need to go very far to be happy either.

He asked him to explain better what he meant and listened to him in awe as he reported the conversations he'd had with his interesting father and his mother who was always there for him, who the younger boy envied to death.

'My mum says that's how happiness works; it happens when you do more with less.'

Friday evening, walking him home, Shūichi insisted on meeting Kenta's parents.

The boy was nervous. Shūichi explained that welcoming him into his house after school in the afternoon was one thing, but taking him all the way to Tōkyō for a whole day was quite another. He would be responsible for his safety, and he couldn't take such a liberty without the approval of his parents.

'But they're fine with it!' Kenta replied, his face darkening.

'Perfect. Then what are you worried about?'

His mother was alone in the house and welcomed Shūichi with extreme politeness. She had just got in and was still wearing an elegant suit, earrings, a necklace, her face flawlessly made-up.

She guided him into the living room and offered

157

him a cup of tea; Kenta disappeared. The woman said she was about to heat up some ready-made food for dinner. She apologised for the untidiness and said work was hellish at the moment. She explained her job, her husband's job, how they managed the house. She spoke without stopping for breath. She seemed focused entirely on the geometry of their lives.

She had known Mrs Ōno well, she said, lowering her voice; she was a lovely woman and she was profoundly grateful for how much she helped Kenta with school. She was very sorry to hear of her death.

Shūichi hurried to say that, unlike his mother, he was not a professional teacher and was only helping the boy when he asked him to. But the woman seemed to know much more about him than Shūichi expected. At the beginning, he was irritated, he felt slightly uneasy about having been studied in such an in-depth way, but then he felt reassured by the thought that Kenta's parents were concerned about how their son was spending his afternoons.

A cloud of concerns later ('Are you sure Kenta won't be a bother?', 'We'd love to have you for lunch one day, as soon as work calms down', 'You

will let me know how much you spend, won't you',
'I don't want to take advantage'), Shūichi excused
himself. He would pick Kenta up at the house the
next morning.

The boy poked his head into the living room
just before the end. Curious as he was, Shūichi
thought, he had probably been listening from behind
the wall.

They walked together to the door, Kenta saying
nothing. Only when Shūichi gave him a pat on the
cheek did he smile.

'It was all fine, you see?' Shūichi whispered as if
it were a secret.

Then he stepped out into the darkness of the road
and put a hand over his heart.

At 09:17, Kenta, Sayaka and Shūichi got on the train
headed for Tōkyō.

Shūichi was nervous but hadn't been able to put
his finger on why.

Kenta and Sayaka played for a long time: they
took out the memory card game, chose twenty pairs,
then twenty-five, then thirty, and laid them out on
the only surface available, Shūichi's satchel. Rather

than the usual animals, the cards had *kanji* on them. They were all to do with parts of the body: eyes, chin, forearm, shoulder blade, stomach.

Shūichi told Sayaka about his mother and Kenta's obsession with *kanji* and it started a conversation about her childhood.

'Apparently as a child I didn't talk at all, apart from when I was alone with my uncle. He was probably the person I liked best. We often went on trips and, as long as I didn't tell anyone, he promised he would teach me the world's secret *kanji*.'

'Secret *kanji*?'

'Yes,' Sayaka smiled, 'he showed me the ancient names of the mountains of Kamakura, of the sea in the Sagami Bay, what a certain intersection was *really* called, a plant that everyone – wrongly – ignored that possessed a phenomenal remedy against greed.'

'Against greed?' Shūichi asked, surprised.

'Yes, I know, it sounds absurd, and what's even more absurd is that I believed everything he told me. My uncle had made all these *kanji* up: he took parts of different characters and stuck them together. Only when I was grown up did I realise it was all his invention.'

Shūichi burst out laughing. 'How did you react when you found out they weren't true?'

'First I was really angry and I threatened not to talk to him any more. But then, almost immediately, I started to laugh and I continued to laugh so much and so loud that still now, when one of them comes into my mind, I burst into laughter.'

'Do you still remember them?'

'Of course, every single one,' Sayaka laughed. 'And they're useless! Utterly useless! An entire part of my memory is occupied by totally redundant knowledge. You know,' she continued, 'I think this is the first time I've told anyone. It was a game that my uncle played only with me, and the pact was that I wouldn't tell anyone. So even after he died, it remained our secret.'

'Your turn!' shouted Kenta in that moment, pulling Sayaka back into the memory card game.

'Right, sorry!'

The train pulled into Shinagawa just as Kenta had one more turn to find the liver and the spleen and Sayaka a couple more turns to get the rectum and the pupil.

During the change of trains, Shūichi observed Sayaka and Kenta out of the corner of his eye. They looked like they'd known each other a long time.

He checked his emails on his phone, calculated the time it would take to get from Kanda to Shibuya where the Pokémon exhibit was. He had even bought the tickets online; he had found them excessively expensive but he wasn't discouraged, even when he discovered that there would be a long wait at the entrance.

He had planned that while he took his panels to his editor Ishii-san, Sayaka and Kenta could wait at the Doutor café just next to the publishing house. He didn't want another author, the press officer, a secretary or anyone else who knew him even just by sight to ask questions. For years, explaining had weighed heavily on him. And, anyway, in this case he wouldn't even know what to say.

They arrived at ten thirty. Shūichi handed in the panels, briefly explained the development of the plot and by eleven fifteen they were on the metro to Shibuya.

The Pokémon exhibit turned out to be marvellous.

Luckily, they didn't have to wait as long as they

expected: after thirty minutes in the queue, they were inside. Shūichi, who knew all the characters, major and minor, and the developments of the storylines, was overcome by a sort of luminous nostalgia.

Between the enthusiastic squeals of Kenta, who pulled him here and there to take photos and find additional information with his phone and the QR codes, Shūichi tried to explain to Sayaka how a Poké Ball worked, the evolution of a Pokémon and who Professor Oak was.

Once they were outside in the teeming streets of Shibuya, Kenta continued to reproduce the supernatural creatures with twitchy movements and sound effects, offering enthusiastic and unrestrained commentary. The corner dedicated to virtual reality had completely absorbed him and in the two hours spent in there the wall between reality and imagination had collapsed entirely.

Shūichi and Sayaka enjoyed Kenta's excitement and Shūichi suddenly remembered a restaurant in a side street between Harajuku and Shibuya where they served gigantic sundaes. It was the biggest dessert you could imagine: five litres of ice cream, whipped cream and delicious toppings, which you needed at least four people to eat. But he was cautious in his promise: in Tōkyō it was often the case that you couldn't find something a second time.

'It was magnificent, but it's probably not there any more,' said Shūichi to Kenta, to avoid disappointment. 'Tōkyō is constantly changing.'

'Let's try anyway!'

When they arrived at the address he remembered, Shūichi ascertained sadly that the restaurant had indeed changed name and the interior had been transformed from gold and silver to pastel colours. But then they saw in the window, between slices of cake and crêpes, the plastic reproduction of the enormous sundae.

It looked even bigger than before: it was covered in trails of cream, chocolate and meringue, adorned with little biscuits in all different shapes and colourful sprinkles; its corners were stuffed with fruit and toasted muesli, and thin slithers of cheesecake and cherry pie. The whole thing was immersed in an avalanche of whipped cream.

Just seeing it was enough to give all three of them the giggles. They couldn't imagine how they would feel afterwards; they would surely leave the shop bent in two with stomach pain.

Euphorically, they entered, ordered loudly and clearly the *Jumbo Parfait*, and for the next hour played Hansel and Gretel, first devouring the mountain of sweetness by the spoonful, then pulling out the harder bits with their fingertips, and finally sucking the melted bits up through straws.

They would feel sick for weeks, but would remember that afternoon forever.

How Kenta, Shūichi and Sayaka crossed the Shibuya Crossing and how that experience made each of them aware of something, something silent, they had inside them

KENTA

Kenta emitted squeaks of excitement at the idea of crossing the Shibuya Crossing, which, according to Shūichi, was the most crowded pedestrian crossing on the planet. He wanted to do it from every side as if it were a racetrack: he took a run-up, changed gear, sprinted parts, hopped on one leg, then the other, and broke into a run when the green light started to flash. Shūichi and Sayaka tried to dissuade him when he wanted to try crossing with his eyes closed, like he did at Kamakura on the big road leading to the Tsurugaoka Hachimangū shrine. The boy felt protected by the crowd that was so much taller than him, people who were moving in at least five different directions but, as if by magic, didn't bump into each other. He felt like part of the undergrowth: the trees stretched up densely and he, a tiny mushroom, grew in their shadows.

Shūichi

Shūichi focused on all the hearts that were beating at that moment and all the faces he saw for a second before they merged together and disappeared forever. The storyless faces of thousands of strangers. He liked to imagine, among the anonymous crowd of Shibuya, men and women who had won impressive competitions, received great recognition, or spent half of their life behind bars. One of the games he played with his mother when he was young, when waiting at the pharmacy, the bank or outside a restaurant, was to look at the faces of people passing by and invent entire existences. Shūichi believed that if he could just pause for a moment and look properly, on those faces stories would appear.

Sayaka

What Sayaka noticed most when she looked at the crowd at Shibuya were the interlaced couples who crossed the intersection diagonally: young, fearless people. She would never have said it out loud, but it was clear to her in that moment that falling in love can only happen in silence and without caution. Her pulse became chaotic; each time she'd started to love someone in the past, it had felt like her heart was losing a handful of beats a week. She'd get to Monday with a dry mouth, no appetite, and the feeling that the world had been sucked into a pair of eyes and a line, the line she traced around the edge of the person she had chosen. Nobody in her family ever suspected she was in love. Not the uncle she adored and who she told more of her secrets to than her parents, nor her brother, who was older than her but, in her eyes, still little. When it came to matters of the heart, Sayaka a treated discretion as if it were a question of life and death: anything others knew about was sure to end, while whatever seed she managed to secrete away in the cavity of her own chest would bloom, unknown to everyone else.

Kenta had desperately wanted a photo next to the statue of Hachiko the dog: he planned to put it into his school report.

Now all three of them were bent over the screen evaluating whether to take another: in the first one, the boy's eyes were closed, and in the second, a finger was covering half of his face.

'I look horrid in photos,' Kenta said.

'It's because you get embarrassed. The best photos are when you don't try to pose.'

They took another four and headed slowly towards the station turnstiles.

'Maeda-san, long time no see!'

Shūichi looked up and saw a plump woman with carefully applied lipstick and straight eyebrows. Who was she?

'Don't you remember me? I'm Koichirō's mum, Shingo's classmate.'

'Oh, of course, how are you?'

'Very well, thank you. How's your wife?'

'I believe she's well.'

'Believe?'

'We have separated.'

Sayaka stayed silent. She instinctively put her hands on Kenta's shoulders, as if looking for some kind of cohesion in the formless thing they were presenting to this stranger.

'Oh, I'm sorry to hear that. You know, just recently Koichirō got all his photos from primary school out and he was saying how much he misses him.'

The boy looked up at Shūichi. Who was this woman?

'Koichirō must be about to start middle school now,' Shūichi said.

'Yes, he's studying for the private Keio school.'

'Congratulations, it's a very good school.'

'Koichirō still remembers Shingo; he said he'll never forget him. And he's keeping his promise. Every so often, he tells me a story about something they did together at school.'

'Thank you,' Shūichi said drily. Was it possible that the woman hadn't noticed Sayaka and Kenta?

'It truly was a terrible tragedy. You know, since then I haven't taken my son to the swimming pool. I'm just happy that at least you won the case. Something like that must never happen again.'

'Thank you.'

Then, as if just noticing their presence, the woman exclaimed: 'I didn't mean to take up your time, sorry!'

'No worries at all.'

'OK, have a lovely day!'

'You too, and best wishes for Koichirō's studies.'

Shūichi, Sayaka and Kenta headed slowly towards the station.

Nobody asked anything. They boarded the Yokosuka Line train that was, unusually, already waiting at the platform. Kenta ran to occupy a table and all three of them sank into the comfortable seats. They piled their bags onto the fourth.

None of them had spoken since the meeting with the stranger. Kenta was exhausted; he immediately closed his eyes and was asleep by the time they passed through Kawasaki.

'Shingo was my son.'

This topic would have to come up at some point and Shūichi knew that if he didn't bring it up himself, Sayaka would never ask.

'What happened to him?'

'An accident; he drowned in a swimming pool.'

'When?'

'Two years ago.'

Shūichi looked out of the window, but the evening was drawing in and soon he'd see only his own face reflected back at him.

'These things happen,' he said calmly. Then he corrected himself: 'No, that's just something people say, but these things don't usually happen. But it did happen, to us.'

Then Sayaka did something that she never did, not even at work when she washed and made up the bodies and had to confront the pain of the relatives: she reached out and took Shūichi's hands in hers.

'I am so sorry,' she said. And she said it because she really meant it.

When Shūichi explained the accident, Sayaka remembered hearing something similar years before, maybe on the news, but she couldn't recall where it happened or the child's age.

Shūichi told her how, that day, Aya, his wife, had taken Shingo to the pool, like she did every Tuesday and Thursday during the summer holidays. The little boy adored swimming, and jumping in the water was the best way to deal with the suffocating heat of the summer. He loved holding his breath for a few seconds, to then pop out at the other side of the pool as if to surprise her. Aya watched him, taking part in his game from the side.

That day, she remembered telling Shingo to get out, then turning around for a few seconds to get his towel and lunch box, and turning back to call him again. She wanted him to eat his *onigiri* and the apple she'd sliced up for him that morning at home. It was almost noon and he was surely hungry; he just didn't realise as he was having so much fun.

When she turned back, however, Shingo wasn't there. Aya searched the dozens of children paddling around in the pool, scoured the surface waiting the three or four seconds it usually took him to re-emerge, but nothing. From one moment to the next, he had vanished from sight.

When she was certain of his absence, Aya shouted for help and jumped into the pool immediately when she spotted his shape under the water. By that point, though, Shingo had already lost consciousness.

He had been sucked down by the aeration pipe, which, due to a malfunction, had held him down on the bottom. The boy had gone almost immediately into cardiac arrest and the repeated cycles of resuscitation on the edge of the pool were no use. He was transported by an emergency helicopter and announced dead at the hospital. You could say he drowned, or that his heart stopped out of fear.

The incident was followed by technical reports to establish who was responsible, the causes of the malfunction, the strength of the aspiration exercised by the pipe, the precise point where Shingo was swimming and the exact dynamics of the event.

In the weeks following 16 August, Shūichi received periodic contact from lawyers. He didn't understand the technical terminology they used to explain his son's death. He felt like he was constantly staring into the sun and moving around blind. He

174

gave his signature when it was needed, but Aya scolded him harshly if he put off responding to an email or phone call even for a few hours: his negligence put the timing of the hearing at risk, breaking the infinite concatenation of cavils that would grant them 'justice'. Shūichi heard that word and didn't understand it: what exactly was *just*? Winning the case?

Aya couldn't forgive herself for having been there the whole time but missing the exact moment that he went under. It was in her nature to apologise for things, even when she knew she wasn't to blame. As a result, fatally, to Shūichi everything sounded like an accusation.

If Shūichi had been there with them at the pool that day, she wouldn't have had to turn around to pick up the towel and the lunch box; she would've been watching her son! If only Shūichi hadn't developed his absurd aversion to chlorine, he would have gone with them and fate would have done another lap! Of course, fate always returns, but dying at eight years old, and in that way! It was too much!

'There's no such thing as fate, for God's sake!' Aya had shouted and slammed the door the day

Shūichi looked, to her, like he'd given up for good.

He, however, stood in the garden, watching those days stretch out their branches and twigs until they covered the entire sky.

The quote Shūichi copied into his notebook on 3 November that year

'I am no longer irritated by the fairy tale's happy end: I need it.'

—ELIAS CANETTI, *THE SECRET HEART OF THE CLOCK*, TR. JOEL AGEE

chapter
two

AYA WAS WELL-PROPORTIONED, BUT VERY small.
She was under a metre and a half tall.

When Shingo was born, Shūichi thought she
looked like a child who had given birth to another
child: a curious set of matryoshka dolls where he
could contain her who had contained a baby. That
image really amused him, so much that one day he
drew three matryoshkas and, without explaining
anything, put them into a square frame and hung it
in the living room.

He remembered what he felt when Aya first came

into his life. Sharing a table in the university canteen; finding her in front of him at the restaurant where they went to eat after class. Aya had immediately occupied a more expansive space in his life than he realised. What did she do when they weren't together? What toothpaste did she use? Did she prefer steamed fish or grilled fish? And surfing? Did she like surfing?

These questions expanded his soul: Shūichi was preparing the space for another person.

The first time he laid his eyes on her, he was nineteen. They were in French class and Aya had bustled in, breathless, just as the teacher was moving students around so they could practise their role play with someone different. There had been a suicide on the Chūo Line that morning and the lesson was interrupted a few times by late students.

The bright blue sky streamed in through the large windows of the fifth floor of the university. Clouds lay along the horizon and Shūichi remembered it was autumn; everything important in his life happened in autumn.

After that day, Aya accelerated, while Shūichi remained still. Two months into their courtship, she said 'I love you' and he was stumped. The same happened years later when she told him she was expecting a child. Shūichi, who didn't trust language, was bewildered by the way what Aya felt corresponded so precisely with what she said.

He believed, on the contrary, that people had things but not the words to say them. The words might have existed, but nobody could find them when they needed them. He imagined someone holding a baseball bat while balls flew past them in the air; or maybe they hit a ball but it never quite reached the point they were aiming for. Shūichi was convinced that in the rare case that someone had the words to say what they meant, it was usually an accident.

But Aya's sentiments seemed to land on him unequivocally, directly.

When Shingo was born, Shūichi was confused like he had never been before. Up to a certain point, he hadn't felt much affection for his son: he was all Aya's; he had no need for Shūichi. He loved him for all his mystery as a newborn baby, but he would have had difficulty saying who *he* was, that child he called, with a false portrayal of comfort, *my son*.

Truthfully, at the beginning Shūichi was mostly terrified. He would never have admitted it, especially not when Aya seemed terrified herself, though for completely different reasons. She was afraid she wouldn't be a good mother, that she wouldn't be able to breastfeed him properly, or be capable of following his development adequately. Shūichi was simply afraid of loving him.

For Shūichi, the birth of a child, like that of any love – a new friendship, a new lover, a colleague you cared for – was a risk.

'The more people you add, the more difficult happiness becomes, because it's no longer enough that things are going well for you, they have to be going well for them too,' he confided once to Doctor Fujita.

'Sure, statistically speaking, extending the range of your affections will decrease your portion of happiness. You'll no longer be 100 per cent happy,' the doctor responded with a smile as he took Shūichi's heartbeat. 'Assuming you were 100 per cent happy before.'

It was the same day the doctor had told him it would soon be time to operate on his heart. He shifted to a quiet, confidential tone.

'I would happily skip the operation,' Shūichi sighed, buttoning up his shirt.

'It's not going to happen immediately, Maeda-san, don't worry. I just don't want you to forget that it will be necessary,' Doctor Fujita said. 'Anyway, it'll be maximum one week in hospital and then we'll get you back to life as usual.'

Shūichi said goodbye to Doctor Fujita and went home. He couldn't have imagined that, just a year after the operation, he'd be back in the cardiologist's office with a brand-new diagnosis: *tako-tsubo*, or broken heart syndrome.

A week after the appointment, the idea of the operation transformed into anguish: Shūichi became paralysed by an urgency to give his family economic stability. That evening after dinner, at the end of a very difficult day (his book idea had been rejected and he'd seen a review that called his most recent publication 'a fall'), Shūichi sat down to work. Aya lay down in bed to get the child to sleep and, as often happened, fell asleep with him.

Sitting at the table observing their four tiny feet at the end of the futon, Shūichi imagined no longer having a family. He erased, like pencil on paper, everything in the house that represented Shingo and Aya: the colourful toys, the flowery bowls, the fabric books, eyeliner, mascara, skirts. One day they would be textbooks, a leather rucksack, food Aya had made for dinner then spent the evening critiquing.

He was tired of communicating so much, so often, with people who slipped from one room in the house to another, as if in boats on swollen seas. That evening, it felt like too much effort to face life in the first person. He had underestimated how much effort it took. The concept of 'family' brought with it a freight of things to do and not do, together and alone; an unending series of yeses and nos.

Shūichi would repeat this game many times over the years, becoming a habit that held no emotional weight. He would just do it, like imagining removing the table from the room and replacing it with a wardrobe.

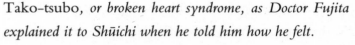

9.

Tako-tsubo, *or broken heart syndrome, as Doctor Fujita explained it to Shūichi when he told him how he felt.*

'*Tako-tsubo*, or broken heart syndrome, is a cardio-myopathy that's usually transitory, caused by acute stress of a physical or psychological origin such as a trauma, bereavement, separation or a situation of extreme danger. Your case is clearly ascribable to your recent bereavement. This syndrome causes the dysfunction of the left ventricle, and presents with symptoms similar to those of a heart attack: pain in the chest, irregular heartbeat, a feeling of suffocating. It is not usually permanent and leads to death in only 1 per cent of cases. But you have an existing heart condition, so you need to find a way to lighten your psychological burden. Do you sleep at night, Maeda-san? Are you eating?'

185

b.

Tako-tsubo, *or broken heart syndrome, as Shūichi read about it later in a book he had at home.*

'*Tako-tsubo,* or broken heart syndrome, was described for the first time in Japan in 1991, and after a 6.8 magnitude earthquake struck the prefecture of Niigata on 23 October 2004, a team of researchers studied sixteen patients who had been diagnosed with it. Its name comes from the Japanese term for an octopus trap, which is similar in shape to a heart affected by this syndrome. The research was carried out on a sample of fifteen women and one man, average age 71.5 years, all survivors of the earthquake. The researchers calculated that the stress caused by the disaster had increased the probability of contracting "broken heart syndrome" twenty-four-fold.'

c.

What Shūichi thought that day, before going to bed.

'So, it's true, you can die from love. You can die from a broken heart.'

More than a thousand children disappear in Japan every year.

Some of them are found, others you just assume have been involved in some sort of accident: plummeted into the sea; tumbled off a mountainside; or, as children often do to feel safe, squeezed into unimaginable hiding places, extremely tight gaps, where, out of sheer bad luck, they eventually perish. And others, poor things, are trafficked into trades the nature of which it is impossible to grasp. And then there are those who run away, which is perhaps the least painful outcome, because they are usually teenagers, almost adults, fourteen, fifteen, sixteen years old, and more often than not they are running from cruelty and neglect.

Shūichi read up on missing children in Japan with the angst of someone who would never be capable of facing such adversity. Love, he repeated to himself, was an intolerable risk. In his most brutally honest moments, he wondered whether that was why he chose Aya, because, yes, he loved her, but not desperately: his life wouldn't stop if she left him.

Over the years, Shūichi had trained his hand to let go of things more than to hold onto them; he had taught himself to do less, to feel less. But a child didn't come into the category of things you could keep under control; certainly not one who came into your life brand new. Starting from a place of crushing superiority – a superiority that was physical and intellectual precisely because of the boy's absolute fragility; adding to it the sense of guilt that highlighted all the ways your own ugliness had inevitably slipped into the creature, defeat was predestined. Then, casting him out into the world without knowing how to teach him to do better than you did, partly because you were incapable, partly because the world was different and what once counted for something was no longer valid. What of any meaning could he ever give to his son?

As a child, Shūichi had good boy syndrome, which transmuted into good husband syndrome. But good father syndrome broke him. He wasn't earning enough from his children's books and, faced with Aya's frustrations, he felt constantly incompetent. He tried his vacuous look, but that didn't work; he told her he would try harder, but he wasn't confident he knew how. Life felt like a constant promise that he would fabricate another life that would be more effective, more secure.

But with Shingo, Shūichi never got it wrong: the child reassured him. Over time, the complicated love that Shūichi had tried so hard to keep at arm's length grew and, when his son began to talk, it exploded.

'You're the best daddy in the world!'

After 16 August, the day of the swimming pool, Aya and Shūichi tried their best.

The first thing Aya did was get a part-time job in their local *konbini*.

'You could do more than that with your skills,' Shūichi had told her.

'There's nothing wrong with working in a convenience store,' she replied.

Aya had actually done a trial week in a restaurant, but she had stopped as soon as the week was over.

She would never forget the stress she had felt while waiting for customers, apron tied tight around her waist, hair pulled back, wandering up and down between empty tables. She had looked out of the windows a thousand times and wondered how many of the people hurrying along the pavement or flying past on bikes alongside the cars felt the same urgent need to escape themselves as she did; how many of them spent their days trying to keep their thoughts at bay.

'I wasn't judging the *konbini* job, it just looks tiring,' Shūichi protested.

'It is. That's why I chose it. I am tired, but I want to see with my own eyes that life is going on. People coming in and going out through the automatic doors, people choosing things to eat, toothbrushes, nylon stockings, fruit ice lollies, people buying cigarettes, alcohol, junk food, paying their bills. I don't want life to leave me in peace; I want it to make an infernal noise, to pull me along by the T-shirt and not give me a moment to think.'

Shūichi didn't reply. He realised that Aya, the child who had become a mother, had regressed to being a child again.

Shūichi's strategy was different.

To save himself, he constructed, in detail, one day that he repeated for months.

Sometimes he concluded that he'd survived thanks to distraction.

'I survived because I was distracted,' he said to Sayaka that afternoon, as the train slipped between the folds of Shibuya and into Kanagawa.

Thanks to distraction, the second arrow didn't end up in his chest, like it would have for William Tell had he misjudged the first shot. Shūichi turned everything off. The energy didn't go to his stomach, nor his chest. He hadn't eaten, hadn't drunk, but neither had he lengthened his stride when the driverless train was about to come through the station. He had tried, instead, to stop everything. He had seen on TV how certain animals froze when they were in pain.

For months, Shūichi had avoided music and television. When one day, he picked up a book on the chemical composition of stones, and the phase Shingo went through of collecting them (and the immense joy he found in putting them into boxes) popped into his mind, he stopped reading books.

191

He had realised, horrified, that Shingo's memory was in everything.

One afternoon when Shingo was six and Shūichi thirty-six

'Let's play riddles!'

'Again?'

'Yes!'

'Come on then, you start!' said Shūichi.

They were walking home from nursery school and Shingo was already trembling with joy. This had been his favourite game for over a month.

'It's a hole but it's also a house, what is it?'

'A burrow!'

'Bravo!'

'That was easy!'

'Again!'

'Go on then!'

'It's soft and white.'

'A cloud?'

'No.'

'A marshmallow?'

'What?'

'The things we melted on the fire at the campsite, remember? They were soft and really sweet.'

Shingo looked thoughtful.

'OK, so do you eat this soft and white thing?'

'No, you can't eat it.'

'And it's not alive?'

'No.'

'A pillow?'

Shingo often gave himself away with his little hands, which, naturally, mimed the things that whirled around in his head.

'Correct!'

'That was hard.'

'Can I do another one?'

'Go on, you can take my turn.'

'This one's easy: animals that lived thousands of years ago.'

'If you're thinking of dinosaurs, you know they didn't live thousands of years ago.'

'One thousand three hundred?'

'They became extinct sixty million years ago.'

'OK. Last one!'

'Go on.'

194

'It's on two legs, has spikes on its back, and blows fire from its mouth.'

Shūichi took a few goes before saying the answer: it was Godzilla.

'I saw it at Grandma's house. It was soooo scary!'

Shingo was still walking like Godzilla as they went into the house.

August was winter and September was both spring and autumn.

When Shūichi came out of his lethargy, his heart had hardened, a cascade of little calcifications spreading between his arteries and other nameless parts. He didn't cry, just stubbornly repeated the same day for an entire year.

He perfected it to the point that hunger and thirst came for the same food and drink, at the same time. Even inspiration for his work was on demand. It was banal, it was boring, but he was convinced that was what he needed. It was the absence of variables, not having to choose anything – not even what to wear (every day he washed the same clothes, a cycle of boxers, jeans and T-shirts to which he simply added or subtracted a layer if it was hot or cold). Not having to decide was what took care of him.

He was obsessive about every detail, careful to not create any kind of variation. On the last day of the month, he assembled all the nuisances: the bills that needed paying, the things that needed organising. On that day each month, he opened his post and, like an automaton, made one phone call after another.

Where he could, he delegated, and he tried not to get sick. The idea of staying in bed for days with flu, breaking his routine, terrified him.

'You look like a robot; you don't speak, you say nothing. I could be on the other side of the world and it would make no difference to you,' Aya accused him one morning.

'I don't understand this life, but I am continuing this life that I don't understand. I'm not trying to change it; I look at it, it doesn't move me,' Shūichi responded calmly, and she said she was leaving.

As Aya searched for another place to live, he remained alone in that house where all three of them had lived in equal parts and that now seemed disproportionate not only to the number of people who lived there, but also to the volume of existence spent there.

Shūichi continued his life that he didn't understand.

He continued not answering the phone, wearing his face mask everywhere just to avoid showing any feeling on his lips. At the *konbini*, he put his pre-cooked bentō, can of coffee and bag of gummy sweets on the counter, handed over his Lawson points card, said the word 'Suica' and the woman behind the counter pointed at the place where he could scan his pre-payment card. It seemed like magic.

His mother looked for him; she phoned him, but he didn't pick up. He wouldn't have known what to say to her, he thought. She then began to send him little cards: watercolours she made herself, picture books in English and French that she ordered directly from the Kinokuniya international bookshop. That was how they had communicated since Shūichi could hold a pencil in his hand. Every week, without asking him or Aya for their permission, Mrs Ōno had a basket of fruit delivered to their house: apples, pears, persimmons in autumn, strawberries and grapes in spring. In those months, Shūichi felt his mother's effort and love. Knowing she was nearby provided great relief, but he knew that no lie of hers would be capable of protecting him from the facts: his happiness was gone.

Every so often, he responded to her with little cards on which he didn't write but he too drew. Sometimes it was a single leaf, other times an empty window, or a bluish apple.

Then, at the start of summer, the lawyer got in touch. It wasn't about the case this time – they'd already won – but the divorce. Shūichi just nodded.

His purpose was to not let himself be overwhelmed by the loss, and in his success, he wondered whether he was heartless, a person who feels nothing, and forgets quickly if he does. Suffering was for people with depth, and he was shallow.

On one of those days, in a gap left unsupervised between lunch and dinner, he realised that no one ever talked about how much this illusory shallowness cost in happiness: it was true that suffering less was equivalent to silencing the pain, but it also meant putting a part of yourself out of use, the same part that, crucially, held the capacity for joy.

It was as if he was sitting at a laid table, his hands gathered in his lap, lavishing polite smiles on those who ate hungrily, passed one another the water; and the only thing that occupied his mind was not working out how to participate in the banquet, but how not to. Shūichi tried desperately not to salivate, to resist the temptation to pass the sauce, or fulfil someone's request to fill their glass with water.

There was nothing he could do: if he renounced pain, joy drained away with it.

In those months, he was convinced that his life would always be like this, until, all of a sudden, everything changed. One day you find a broken key in the lock, a strange boy comes into your house, and the hope you thought had gone, like a forgotten habit, returned.

Shūichi smiled as he said it.

On the train from Shibuya to Kamakura, winter seemed to have returned. The sky turned leaden; the wind sharpened the landscape.

'That's when I understood that this is the price you pay not to suffer, and not suffering is all you get out of it,' Shūichi concluded.

They were almost at their destination. Kenta, sleeping, had laid his head on Sayaka's arm and then slipped onto her lap.

'I think the realisation you've come to is precious.'

'He helped me too, in his way,' he said, nodding towards Kenta.

When Shūichi had read Kenta's list for how to face being eight years old (he had taken a photo, and he showed it to Sayaka on his phone), he initially thought the boy imaginative, then turned silent.

The same happened one afternoon when Kenta got to the house triumphant: he had picked his job for when he grew up!

'And so, what will you be?'

'I'll be a novelist,' he declared.

'Why?'

Why? Wasn't it obvious? So he could tell as many fibs as he liked! But also because he'd found out that he could watch himself living, practise being outside of himself.

He said the word 'outside' at least a dozen times.

'And you think that would make you happy?' Shūichi had asked with the least concern he could muster.

'Of course, then you don't have to feel any of the horrible stuff!'

As the weeks passed, a vague sadness took hold of him.

It was true that Kenta dreamed aloud, that he created fantastical adventures as he walked along the streets, but in reality he did nothing to make them come true. He extracted himself from everything: family meals, games with the other kids at school.

'He must have been excluded at first, and then decided to distance himself from everything, like an extreme form of self-defence,' Shūichi said to Sayaka, who was looking at him attentively.

Here it was, 'the irony of fate', thought Shūichi. It had been knocking at his door for weeks, ever since that strange boy had sneaked into the garage and gradually crossed the threshold and settled himself into the armchair.

'Kenta has placed in front of me all the strategies I have been using since my own childhood, everything I invented to avoid needing things or people,' said Shūichi.

He watched the sky turning black outside.

'It's just that, by going without, I have limited what I can feel. And now I look around me and suddenly I'm nothing.'

'What do you mean?' Sayaka interrupted. 'To me, you look like a well-respected artist.'

The roles, the names that had pulled him into the world, said Shūichi, had disappeared forever: he was no longer a *father*, or a *son*, or a *husband*. Who knew if he could even call himself a *friend*.

'The truth is that we never have an absolute value. Nothing and no one has an absolute value. We are who we are thanks to the names we are called in the world, the roles we carve out for ourselves in the lives of others,' whispered Shūichi.

That's why when, one afternoon some weeks before while watering the pine in the garden, Kenta asked him: 'Are you my friend?' Shūichi, who was never emotional, who hadn't even cried at his own son's funeral, nor his mother's, said, 'Of course. Sorry, wait there a minute . . .' and ran into the house. Kenta stood there waiting as Shūichi, locked in the bathroom, sobbed.

'When we cry, we save ourselves a little: you told me that at my mother's funeral. Do you remember?'

'I don't remember.' Sayaka shook her head. 'But I could have done . . . you seemed like someone who didn't let go enough. For a man who had lost his mother, you were too controlled.'

'You said it just like this: "when we cry, we save

ourselves a little",' Shūichi repeated, convinced.

Those words had the sound of Sayaka's voice inscribed on them and perhaps that was why, each time he met her, the thought of this woman was so precious.

He'd forgotten her every time, it was true, but every time he bumped into her, he had felt happy, had experienced a sense of well-being, like when you bump into a childhood friend.

'In the end, it was your words that stopped me from being ashamed of how I cried that afternoon. It has only happened to me one other time, before I left Tōkyō. The day, I think, that I started processing the grief of losing my son.'

He didn't explain what happened *that day* and Sayaka, after a few seconds, said: 'You did well. And, anyway, there's no wrong way to cry.'

As if she had just remembered, she added: 'I think our roles in life are continuously changing. Perhaps we don't remain children of the same people, nor parents or spouses. Look at me: my uncle was like a father to me. I never understood my parents. I loved them but I never felt in tune with them. It was my uncle who parented me, who gave me the kind of guidance that makes a child feel important and loved.'

Sayaka stopped to take a breath and Shūichi realised he had never heard her talk for that long before.

'I am nobody's mother, but I am sure that more than once, accompanying people in their mourning, I have played that role. I don't know, maybe it sounds confusing, but I believe we can rebuild ourselves, a little each day.'

Shūichi remained silent.

'And,' whispered Sayaka, 'look at this child . . .'

The train left Ōfuna and the next stop was announced: Kita-Kamakura. Just two stations left. Sayaka gently moved Kenta's head.

'We should wake him,' she said softly.

'Kenta! We're here!' announced Shūichi, taking the boy's still-sleeping face in his hands. 'Oh well,' he said and, handing Sayaka the rucksack, gathered Kenta up in his arms.

What happened the day Shūichi started to process the grief of losing his son

It started with a dream about a child curled up, no bigger than a fist, at the bottom of an empty swimming pool. Since then, all of Shūichi's dreams involved water: ferry journeys, small boats on the lake, pirate ships.

Then, one morning, he woke up drenched in sweat and felt a rage, not so much with life as with the idealised celebration of the *perfect* boy who was killed by the *damned* malfunctioning of the *goddamned* aeration pipe of that *stupid* swimming pool in Tōkyō.

He resisted this celebration, and that's how he saved the memory of his son.

Because Shingo was also the boy who farted under the duvet and waited for his dad to come and lift it up and laughed at the same outraged words he said every time; who shouted with all his might if there was something on his plate that he didn't like; who

206

made him feel ashamed when he was tiny, rolling around in the street howling because his father refused to buy him a new toy.

And as he laughed about those things, things that in the moment had made him froth with rage, Shūichi realised it was the concreteness of his son, his being trivial and impossible, that moved him most. 'Fuck off!' he counted one thousand seven hundred and eighty times; he too playing at counting things like Shingo loved to do.

That day, he regained the desire to feel.

He realised that what he missed wasn't so much the backdrop – the house, the school, the weekends spent as a family doing the things they always did. It was, rather, a detail dropped randomly into conversation, a tiny object found around the house, a stupid face being pulled.

After laughing, Shūichi cried. He cried in front of the toothbrush left on the sink, stroking its bristles how he once stroked the tip of Shingo's tiny nose. The bookmark in his son's history book saddened him, as did the one in his literature book: he found bookmarks in different colours in the book for each subject. He cried because there, time had stopped, and Shingo's bookmarks revealed how much he liked moving forward through time.

That day when he left the house, Shūichi started to see people, trees, the air again. He bought something different to eat, he even ventured into a restaurant. He was cautious about many things, but the courage he found in remembering Shingo's silliness was surprising.

In the evening, after months of not doing it, Shūichi resumed the ritual he had held since he was a child. He picked up the stethoscope his mother had given him and listened to his heart.

chapter
three

'To be happy, first of all you need to imagine being happy.'

That's what Mrs Ōno taught her son; it was what she had learned herself as a child, spending long days on her own. She was so convinced of it that she would tell anyone who would listen; she would get up on a stage, stop people on the street and tell them: 'Happiness often starts with a lie. And if you insist on believing it, it becomes true.' That's what she used to say.

'And did you believe her?'

'Shouldn't I have?' Shūichi laughed.

One week after the trip to Shibuya, Sayaka and Shūichi sat on the train heading to Enoshima. They were going to the aquarium because Shūichi needed to look at jellyfish up-close. He was working on the illustrations for the bit where the little protagonist of his book goes fishing under the sea.

'I haven't been to Enoshima aquarium since I was a little girl, if you want company,' Sayaka had offered. And so, the next morning, they took the local Enoden train from Kamakura and, at Hase station where the tourists got off in droves, Sayaka took his hand. Shūichi caressed it gently with the same fingers he had used all night to draw, and wash his boxers and socks.

As Sayaka spoke, Shūichi remembered when he had started to see his ex-wife and the imprudence with which he told her everything that passed through his head. 'I don't understand,' Aya would say, and there would be a kind of melancholy in her voice. Looking at Sayaka's profile, Shūichi promised himself that, if their story were to continue, he wouldn't make the same mistake again. He tried to steer the conversation elsewhere.

But Sayaka continued: 'I like your mother's idea. In fact,' she reflected out loud, 'a lesson at school, a business meeting, a family gathering — if you really get into the role of an enthusiastic person, everything does feel more joyful.'

Shūichi looked at her and thought that she had the brightest eyes he had ever seen.

'Sometimes even love starts with a lie . . . but then becomes true with time. Right? Like in school, a boy gets a crush on a girl just because he's been told that she likes him.'

'Has that ever happened to you?' Shūichi asked jokingly.

'All the time,' Sayaka laughed.

When they arrived at Enoshima, the sun was already high in the sky. They walked down the restaurant-lined street that led to the wide boulevard that runs along Sagami Bay. Sayaka couldn't resist a giant rice cracker and had to eat it quickly because you weren't allowed to eat or drink inside the aquarium.

They bought tickets and Shūichi said he would have liked to bring Kenta. He had seemed quiet since the trip to Shibuya.

'He laughs less, and stares into space a lot. I'm a bit worried . . .' Shūichi said.

'He's growing up, that's all,' Sayaka observed as they climbed the blue steps to the entrance.

'Hmm, maybe.'

As they entered, Sayaka's heart began to beat differently. She noticed immediately.

Could it be? she wondered. And in the next moment, they plunged, hand in hand, into the darkness of the aquarium.

Around them were only children and fish.

*The research that Sayaka read two days
before in the library that made her wonder
'Could it be?' when, standing next to Shūichi,
her heartbeat seemed to change*

Scientists at the University of California have discovered that the hearts of people who are in love beat in unison if they sit opposite one another and gaze into each other's eyes. In love, the hearts of women adapt more quickly to the rhythm of their companion.

More recent research at the University of Illinois, coordinated by Brian Ogolsky and published in the *Journal of Social and Personal Relationships* confirmed that a person's heart rate tends to synchronise with that of their lover, especially in couples who have been together for a long time. The results of the study, based on a sample of couples over the age of sixty-five – who wore sensors that measured their heart rate and the physical distance from their partner at various points in the day for a period of two weeks – clearly demonstrated this self-regulation of heartbeats.

They come together, like in a dance.

While Shūichi was looking at the tanks, scanning the depths in search of crabs and starfish, wandering into the jellyfish centre, and finally sitting down to draw, he had a distinct sense that Shingo was there with him.

In his dreams, his son lived sea adventures, always surrounded by water, almost as if he had turned into a fish.

Shūichi drew, and suddenly the room was filled with children, mingling in the purplish darkness, pressing their hands and noses against the glass panes, their giggles filling the air. Shingo darted among the tails of sharks and eels, emerged as a reflection in the trails of rays, happily puffed up his cheeks as he surfaced with the jellyfish. Shingo was in the ocean under the surfboards, in every sea or lake on the planet, in the tanks of all the world's aquariums; he was even there in the mineral water served at the French restaurant and in the cup of tea Shūichi drank before bed. A supernatural creature, Shingo, his beloved boy-fish, would live forever.

Shūichi allowed himself to feel moved only when Sayaka walked away to see the otters. He was happy, and page after page of his sketchbook was filled with jellyfish.

After two hours immersed in the darkness of the aquarium, they emerged into the sunlight. They rubbed their eyes and laughed loudly. They took the train home and Sayaka squeezed his hand again. They hardly spoke.

When the train pulled in to Kamakura, it had just gone two o'clock. They said a brief goodbye in front of the station and, as usual, made no promises. Perhaps, thought Shūichi as he walked home, the desire to see each other again lies precisely in this uncertainty.

Shūichi quickened his pace. He was worried that Kenta would have already left school and be waiting for him.

Crows scrutinised the bins from the rooftops and, around the bend, Shūichi spotted Kenta's brown, tousled head. He was rocking back and forth like a little robot.

Kenta looked so fragile, it scared Shūichi. It seemed like the boy would give anyone the power to change him – for better or worse, it didn't matter.

'Hey!' he shouted as Kenta, who must have climbed up to the Concubine's Tunnel several times, was coming down the hill again. 'Sorry, I came as fast as I could. I was at Enoshima, at the aquarium.'

'Jellyfish?'

'Yes, jellyfish.'

'Was it a good trip?' Kenta asked politely.

'Very good.'

Shūichi opened his bag and flipped through the sketchbook full of jellyfish. He had drawn them in pencil in a variety of positions.

'I like this one,' Kenta said, pointing at a small, round jellyfish. 'It looks like a balloon.'

'And you? How was school?' asked Shūichi.

'It's the holidays soon, and this year I want to write something really brilliant for my project. But I don't know if my parents can take me on a trip.'

216

'Where would you like to go?'

'I don't know, I need to think about it.'

'And the *kanji* test? Wasn't it today?' asked Shūichi.

'Tomorrow.'

'Come on, let's go and study then. Are you hungry?'

While Shūichi prepared pancakes with strawberry jam, Kenta wrote the stroke order of the *kanji* in his notebook. They sat down together at the small table, and Shūichi dedicated himself entirely to the boy. Shūichi explained the origins and together they made up stories to help Kenta memorise the characters and their phonetic variations.

'Are you not doing your things today?' asked Kenta.

'I worked enough this morning,' Shūichi reassured him; he had worked the night before as well.

Kenta saw that he was tired but didn't say anything. When Shūichi fell asleep in his chair while waiting for him to finish his page, Kenta didn't wake him up. The boy silently watched him from his own chair and noticed something in Shūichi's face, in that pose of abandon that he had never seen before, that filled him with a sensation he couldn't understand. He felt

217

it growing every day since they had gone to Shibuya together. He wanted to get rid of that thought, wake Shūichi up immediately and tell him everything. But fear won. Because Shūichi hated lies, so he would probably hate him too.

Kenta remained still at the table, pencil suspended in mid-air. With his other hand, he pressed his left pocket, where for two years he had kept the key to his good fortune.

The boy lowered his eyes to his notebook and suddenly knew that what he was feeling was sadness. A sadness so immense it cast a shadow over the whole earth.

That evening, hours after Kenta had gone home and was already asleep, Shūichi and Sayaka exchanged some messages. Thank you for a lovely morning, she wrote. Thank you to you, he replied. Sayaka wrote that she had been thinking about the conversation they'd had on the train all day. One day, she wrote, she would tell him the story of her uncle, of his secret family, of her cousin who she had only met as an adult, and how her brother Aoi had met Mio, her sister-in-law. They too were proof that everything could start from a lie; what mattered was only where it ended up.

'The end doesn't care how things start,' Sayaka wrote. 'Faith is the only thing that makes a difference: if you believe in happiness enough to imagine it, eventually it will come.'

Smiling at the thought, they finally said goodnight and Shūichi fell asleep.

That night, Kenta had a fever.

doki doki

'Who's your favourite person in your family?'

'My mum, because we like the same things, like manga and TV series. My dad's hardly ever there, but it's nice when he is. You?'

'I don't know. I like them both. My mum does everything for me, like making me the food I like and hugging me a lot. But my dad teaches me a ton of things and we draw pictures together.'

'Who's your favourite Pokémon?'

'Mew, because it can make itself invisible.'

'I like Pikachu, because it's nice to everyone, even strangers.'

'You're nice too.'

'Only with people I know. I'm scared of strangers.'

'I'm also rubbish at being nice to people who scare me, I always hide or look away. Like my swimming teacher . . . she scares me sometimes.'

The younger boy felt happy. He accepted defeat since it was the older boy who inflicted it upon him. And being united over something, similar even in something ugly, made that something suddenly feel more fair.

He would've done anything to be more like the older boy.

Kenta fell ill on Monday night, and on Thursday, not seeing him after school for the third consecutive day, Shūichi went to his house and rang the doorbell. It was spring now, and the garden was full of tulips and dandelions.

A woman opened the door and looked at him questioningly. Shūichi momentarily wondered if he was perhaps at the wrong house, but he explained who he was and asked after Kenta. The woman was a volunteer from the Kamakura Family Support Organisation. Kenta's parents, she explained, couldn't take time off work and had asked for help keeping an eye on their sick child.

'It's nothing serious, I hope . . .' Shūichi said.

'Just a bout of flu, but his fever isn't going anywhere,' the woman replied thoughtfully. 'If you'd like to say hello to Kenta, maybe you can come back tonight when Mrs Ogawa is here.'

'Thank you,' Shūichi said, and, with a bow, took his leave.

In the days that followed, Shūichi felt as unhappy as he had for a long time.

He was worried about Kenta's health, but what troubled him most was his absence. He went back to Kenta's house, this time taking punnets of strawberries, jars of chestnut jam which Kenta loved, comic books and postcards. But each time, he was told that Kenta was asleep or not up to seeing visitors. He occasionally heard his tiny voice in the background, broken by coughing, and one day Shūichi had the strange sensation that the child was spying from the hallway when he and his mother exchanged their usual greetings.

Then Kenta got better and went back to school, but he still didn't show up in the afternoons. Shūichi became gloomy: he missed the child but, deep down, hoped that it was because maybe, thanks to the illness, Kenta had found a new connection with his parents. Or that, at school, he had learned how to nurture friendships and ignore the two kids who constantly picked on him. He convinced himself that he had been replaced, with the abrupt swiftness with which children develop survival mechanisms.

But the silence remained, the clear sensation that Kenta was avoiding him; the change in atmosphere — now he was certain — had started after the day in Shibuya. What had happened? What had unsettled him? Why this sudden coldness? Hypotheses crowded Shūichi's mind, but he held them back for fear of making things more complicated. When, one afternoon, he spotted Kenta's silhouette in the distance, and Kenta, upon noticing him, slowed down, then turned around, Shūichi was deeply upset. He even began to scold himself for becoming too attached to the child: he had spent years carefully avoiding too much emotion, but now he had failed.

Shūichi left the house before the sun came up the next morning. He got his surfboard out and loaded it onto the bicycle. He rode down to the beach, the air smelling of spring, until he could see nothing but the sea. It felt like the first day on earth.

The best thing to do about Kenta, he thought

hours later, on his way home, was probably to do nothing.

That evening, passing by the fruit shop, he didn't buy strawberries. He bought plums instead.

The postcard Kenta drew for Shūichi (which depicted Loretto the bear drawing his own picture), which he never ended up giving him

Then, one evening, midway through April, it started to snow.

The news spoke of nothing else: a low-pressure front had brought an entire year's worth of snow to the mountains around Tōkyō, Hokkaido's Sea of Okhotsk had frozen over again, and the newly blossomed cherry trees were blanketed in white.

On that surreal night, when the snow showed no sign of stopping, Shūichi bumped into Sayaka.

The snow had halted train services between Ōfuna and Zushi, and in Kamakura the bells on the level crossings rang out in vain. The lights flashed and the barriers remained down, putting a stop to traffic and people.

Sayaka and Shūichi coincidentally found themselves at the same point in the city, near the police station in Ōmachi. They spotted each other among the crowd waiting at the lowered barrier. They smiled, surrounded by people huddled in spring jackets, all asking the same questions over and over: When will they clear the tracks? Why won't they let us cross?

'What are you doing here?'
'Walking. I like it.'

Sayaka knew all the railway crossings by heart and ever since she was a child, she enjoyed counting how many steps before or after her the level crossing would open or close. She would start counting from a distance and conscientiously not speed up or slow down, in order to accurately scrutinise her own fate.

'It's a game I used to play with my father and brother, at least until the accident. A man was hit by a train very close to them, and since then, my brother Aoi has been nervous around level crossings. He's never said it, but I know it's true. He's one of those people with good intentions who worries a lot about things like how to save the world, or the souls of his fellow citizens,' Sayaka smiled.

They were standing side by side, just a few metres

from the barrier and the light that flashed intermittently through the falling snow.

'Are you very different?'

'Me and my brother? Yes, very different, but we're similar when it comes to the important things.'

A boy approached the barrier, smiled hesitantly, and climbed over. He crossed the tracks, and the horn of a train, motionless just up the track, sounded in reprimand.

'And you? What are you doing here?' Sayaka asked.

'Been having trouble sleeping of late. I've found going for a walk in the evening helps.'

'Thoughts?'

Shūichi shrugged.

The restoration took a good half an hour, then finally the train glided towards Zushi, and the barrier was raised.

'Shall we go and get a drink?'

They wandered for a long time, but all the bars in Kamakura seemed to be closed due to the weather. They found a tiny grilled-meat restaurant on a side street off Komachi-dōri. The owner lived on one of the snow-blocked train lines and had given up on the

idea of going home that night. The paper lantern remained lit, casting a quivering scarlet glow over the
black and white of the street.

They ordered drinks and waited for their bodies
to warm up.

'You look sad – what happened?' Sayaka asked.

'Various things . . .'

'Start with one,' she insisted.

The waitress placed two beers and two plates –
one of boiled edamame beans and one of peanuts
– on the table.

'Sometimes,' Shūichi said, 'I imagine going back
to my childhood home, where I live now, but in a
different time, two or three years ago, when my
mother was still alive. Just to talk to her and ask her
about one thing at a time.'

'What would you tell her?' Sayaka inquired.

'I've thought about it a lot. I think the main thing
I would tell her is that I desperately need to know
that I suffered as a child; that I went through some
terribly tough things, but that I managed to overcome
them. That, despite everything, I've grown up.'
Shūichi looked down, rubbing his knuckles. 'You
see, I'm not interested in the rest any more, I'm not

even angry about the lies she told.'

A melancholic song played in the background, contrasting with the lively atmosphere of the restaurant.

'I think your mother lied about your past, erased the sad memories and created cheerful ones in their place, just to ensure you had a kind of reserve of happiness,' Sayaka said softly. 'You know, like food supplies for a long journey, something you keep in your rucksack and use a little as and when you need it.'

'Yes, I'm sure that's true. But you understand that it's useless for me to have been happy in the past. What would actually help me now, the only thing that could make me feel better, is knowing that I can come out of a moment like this, if only because I've done it before.'

Shūichi longed for his childhood, because being a child meant experiencing that exact fear, feeling totally and hopelessly in despair, and the next moment, still bleeding, getting up, smiling and running to play again.

'Heartbreaks, failed exams, friends who disappointed me. I would be satisfied just knowing that I had some desolate, gloomy periods, like teenagers do. I don't remember anything, and what I do remember is confusing. But I remember that I tried to hide my sadness, in the same way my peers hid their crushes,' Shūichi laughed.

A group of young people came into the restaurant. The way the snow fell now seemed joyful, and that joy was infectious. Shūichi and Sayaka watched them as they shook the water off their jackets and settled in around the counter, chatting loudly. The smell of food soon filled the restaurant.

'I don't have children,' Sayaka said. 'I'm not saying this to justify anything . . . but the way I see it, becoming a parent is a bit like embarking on an announced shipwreck. If it's not the waves, it's something else: the wind, the people you meet along the way, the rough sea. Everything seems so complicated that no matter how hard you try, no matter how careful you are, you'll still end up in the water at some point.'

'A shipwreck . . .' Shūichi smiled.

'Your book . . .'

'The publisher didn't really like it, you know. My plan was to eliminate all the characters and be alone for a while.'

Sayaka chuckled. 'How funny, you're the opposite of what you'd expect from a children's book illustrator.'

The chatter of the group blended with the gentle songs the owner selected one by one.

'It's because adults idealise children. We think of them only as small, good, and simple. But children are much more complicated and melancholic than we adults think. Their thoughts can be dark, they face hell just like we do, with the only difference being that they have fewer tools to deal with it. And those incredible tools they do have – irrationality, boundless imagination, the ability to laugh at the silliest things and endlessly repeat the same joke – tools that could give them a real advantage, aren't accepted by us adults. Think about it: children are only taken seriously when they are rational, clear, and explain themselves well . . . basically, when they are not being children.'

Shūichi wondered where the conversation would end. Sometimes he found himself talking without knowing where he was going.

'Children suffer, but often they don't know why, they can't articulate it. And even if they do, they don't believe it's true.'

233

LAURA IMAI MESSINA

Shingo hadn't been a sadder child than the others – if anything, he was unscrupulous. Yet now, upon reflection, every minute of suffering his son had experienced seemed unacceptable to Shūichi.

He thought about Kenta: why was he behaving this way? What had saddened him?

Various hypotheses began to swim around his mind again, but he pushed them away. He told himself, as he did in moments of confusion, that taking them seriously, delving into each one, would only magnify the problem.

'Children are a mystery to me. I watch them, but I don't know how to talk to them, how to play with them. My brother and his wife are trying to have a child, and I'm ashamed to say that the idea of having a child in the house scares me a bit,' Sayaka confessed.

'But you and Kenta got along right away,' Shūichi replied. 'I think it's just a matter of respecting their different way of being. Adults often view childhood as a kind of illness: it'll pass sooner or later, we tell ourselves. Aya used to say the same. I don't blame her for it; in fact, I think she was a wonderful mother. But she also believed that childhood was an illness.

234

Like everyone else, she thought that one day, the often incomprehensible and whimsical creature that Shingo was would be cured: he would become aware of dangers, of the passing time; he would learn to navigate the world with more logic, speak more softly, be less easily bewitched.'

Shūichi remembered the superpowers Shingo was convinced he possessed. How he and Aya had laughed about them.

'I had never thought of childhood as an illness . . .'

'Well, it isn't,' said Shūichi, 'but we adults find relief in believing that sooner or later it'll pass, which means we end up thinking it's not worth the effort of trying to understand it. At most, we learn to live with it, reluctantly.'

'And so? What can we do?'

'It's all wrong. The whole reasoning is wrong. The child is exactly that, a child, and yes, they will disappear; their brain will never again dream in that way, express happiness with that enthusiasm, or be afraid to the point of standing frozen in front of the best and worst things in the world. But childhood is not the age of unconsciousness. It isn't! It's no less important than what comes after!'

235

Shūichi knew it and he had sought every possible opportunity to spend time with Shingo. He drew inspiration from him for his stories, stealing his ideas. 'Can I have them?' he would ask, and Shingo would laugh, close his eyes as if blinded by the sun, and in return ask for a piggyback or for Shūichi to buy him a Chupa Chups or a bag of gummy sweets.

'My brother loved Chupa Chups too,' said Sayaka. 'Actually, his childish side hasn't gone anywhere: he still sucks on them and he's nearly forty. Between us, I find it quite embarrassing at work.'

Shūichi imagined an undertaker with a lollipop in his mouth and laughed.

'Perhaps it's his way of holding onto the happiness of childhood. Our mother spoiled him rotten.'

'But children are often not happy. It's adults who impose happiness upon them. They don't remember how tough it was, or they remember it being much easier than their lives now. They completely misjudge the perspective, forget the proportions, and idealise it simply because they no longer possess it.'

'But Kenta is happier now, Shūichi. I know you were talking about something else, but that counts for something.'

236

Shūichi squinted his eyes. They were burning, and he could feel the exhaustion of the day creeping in.

'I never told you,' Sayaka continued, 'but I had already seen Kenta on the streets of Kamakura. There are lots of children around here who walk home from school on their own, but I remember thinking that this child had one of the saddest faces in the world. He wasn't the only one, of course, but I was struck by the way he played by himself. It took me a while to recognise him because, afterwards, I always saw him with you, and with you, his face was completely different.'

Shūichi felt moved. He had never truly considered the possibility that he could brighten Kenta's days. Yet that was what was happening, and he realised how much good their friendship was doing for them both.

'Childhood can be awful,' he whispered.

'But that wasn't the case for you,' Sayaka replied, looking him in the eye. 'And it wasn't the case for him either.' She took his hands, just as she had done weeks before on the train. 'You are creating a piece of Kenta's childhood. It's true, he's not your son, and it's painful that you didn't have the chance to do it with Shingo. But this child has adopted you, and you have adopted him. I think it's a wonderful thing.'

'Kenta has two parents who love him.'

'I'm sure that's true, but parents can't do everything, and if it were me, I would be grateful to anyone who made my child happy, especially if I was unable to.'

'I don't know,' Shūichi murmured. 'Something changed after Shibuya. He became quieter . . .'

'Yes, you mentioned it before,' Sayaka replied.

'Then he got that fever, and since then, he has disappeared.'

'Disappeared?'

'I went to see him several times, but I never actually saw him. And he hasn't been coming to my place, not after school or at the weekends.'

Sayaka frowned. 'That's strange. Have you tried talking to him about it directly?'

'How? He won't even walk past me on the street.'

'Something must have happened. Talk to him, Shūichi! Don't behave like him. Go and visit him, help him get through this rough patch. I'm sure he feels as unhappy as you do right now.'

'I don't think I can do that.'

'Shūichi, you're the adult. Teach him to resolve things, not to avoid them.' Sayaka gently stroked his knuckles. 'And don't avoid them yourself.'

Some of the superpowers Shingo was convinced he possessed

At three years old:
- a) He could stick his index finger up his nose to make his mother turn around;
- b) He could laugh really loudly to make the soot sprites hiding in the bathtub disappear.

At four years old:
- a) He could stare at the crows to understand their secret language;
- b) He could imagine the Calanda monster next to him when he opened doors at night to drive away the Darkness.

At six years old:
- a) He could sneeze to call his father, wherever he was, just with the power of thought;
- b) He could run to make time go faster;

c) In particular, he could run to make summer
come sooner.

That night, for the first time, Shūichi and Sayaka slept together.

They left the restaurant after midnight in silence. He held her hand tightly, slipped it into his pocket, and led her through the snow. They kissed just inside the Concubine's Tunnel, while the coldest spring night there ever was raged outside.

They entered the house and as he silently undressed her, feeling Sayaka's fingers on the wound in the centre of his chest, and her fingertips running over his trench, Shūichi thought that this was the kind of love that perhaps didn't reconcile you with life, but, temporarily at least, gave it meaning.

It was slow and clumsy; both were hindered by anticipating each other's movements. They were like two children who had entered the woods in search of fireflies and, startled by the night, become frightened.

They held each other tight, clinging to something they perceived in the other but neither of them knew they had inside themselves.

After making love, still wrapped in the blankets, Sayaka pressed her ear against Shūichi's chest. He was about to say something, but she quieted him: 'Let me listen.'

After a few seconds, she spoke again. 'Did you know there's a place where they record heartbeats?'

'What do you mean?'

'It's a kind of library that stores the sounds of people's hearts. It's an archive but also a work of art. I'm simplifying it, but that's the general idea,' Sayaka said. 'Considering your obsession with hearts, I thought you might like it.'

'Dr Fujita, my cardiologist, might have mentioned once . . . I don't really recall. Where is it?'

'It's on a small island in Kagawa Prefecture, in the Inland Sea of Japan. I think the artist who came up with it collected the heartbeats of tens of thousands of people from all around the world.'

'But how?' Shūichi asked.

'During his exhibitions, people could record

their own and listen to those of others. But Japan is the only place where you can hear them all now.'

'Fascinating,' Shūichi whispered, and suddenly remembered Dr Fujita telling him about a museum, the only one in the world, where you could listen to the heartbeats of strangers; a tiny building in a remote location.

'I find it beautiful,' Sayaka said, sitting up. 'Would you like to go?'

'Maybe, yes . . . I imagine it would have a certain effect on me.'

'Ah, Teshima! That's what it was called, Teshima.'

Shūichi sat up as well, running a hand through his hair. The room was filled with the smell of Sayaka's skin. It was a fragrance he would now recognise anywhere, like the scent of honey in a field or May plums.

From the light filtering through the window, Sayaka saw that the snow had stopped.

'Where do you keep your stethoscope?' she suddenly asked.

Shūichi leaned across and opened the drawer of the nightstand.

'It's actually called a phonendoscope, but I prefer

stethoscope too. It sounds much nicer,' he said.

Sayaka smiled. 'May I?'

She confidently placed it around her neck. It looked like a necklace: the earpiece, the tube, and the bell that divided her chest and abdomen into parts. She scanned the room, unsure where to place the chest piece.

'There was a time when Shingo listened to the heartbeat of everything,' Shūichi said. 'Like the table, the windows, the forks.'

Sayaka burst into laughter.

'Really! It was an obsession. I think he did it to honour my interest in his heart. I used to listen to his heartbeat along with mine every evening.'

Sayaka positioned the diaphragm on her chest. She handed the earpieces to Shūichi. 'You once told me that you had never listened to my heartbeat and that it meant we didn't really know each other that well.'

'That's true.'

'Listen now, and tell me what sound it makes.'

'In what language?'

'In all the languages you know.'

The sound of a heart beating in all the languages Shūichi knew

'In Afrikaans it goes *doef doef*, in Albanian *pam pam*, *bam bam*, in Arabic *tum tum*. In Basque it has tons of variations, like *bun bun-bun*, *danba danba*, or *pal pal*; when it beats hard, it goes *punpa* and nervously *panp panp*.'

'Like in Japanese, it goes *doki doki* when we're excited! And then *toku toku* when the beat is calm and *doku doku* when the sound is loud and the heart is anxious.'

'But the neutral sound of a heartbeat is *dokun dokun*.'

'It's true . . .'

'Not to mention the sound of the heart when it's tight with emotion . . .'

'*Kyun*. But also *dokin* or *dokkun dokkun*.'

'They're endless.'

'Anyway, continue telling me how it sounds in other languages.'

'So, in Bulgarian it goes *tup tup*, in Mandarin

Chinese when the heart is calm, it goes *tong tong* and when it's excited *peng peng*, in Dutch *boenk boenk*, *boem boem*, *klop, klop* and in Danish *dunk dunk, bank bank*. In Estonian it sounds like *tuks tuks*, in Italian *tu tump*. The French say *boum boum*, the Germans *ba dumm, bumm bumm, poch poch*. The voice of the heart for the Greeks is *duk duk*, for the Koreans *dugeun dugeun* and *kung kung*. In Hebrew it goes *bum búm* and in Thai *toop toop*.'

'There's so many . . .'

'Shingo and I memorised almost all of them.'

'In Spanish?'

'*Bum bum bum, tucutún tucutún.*'

'In Russian?'

'*Tuk-tuk.* And in Polish *bum bum, bubum* and in Portuguese *tun tum*. Some sound very similar, but the pronunciation is always a bit different.'

'It's very sweet if you think about it.'

'What?'

'We all have one in our chest, all of us. But everyone hears it differently.'

247

Part Three
どきどき doki doki

Only poets, like children, know how to speak the truths that one soon learns to keep silent.

—MAURICE PINGUET

Teshima, Winter
豊島　冬

THE SEASONS VANISH AS SOON as they begin. They are never again full summers, autumns, springs or winters. They are rather approximations, attempts to fulfil the descriptions given of them. And so the sky breaks down, unable to decide which light to host or which wind to blow.

Dr Fujita looks at the sea of Teshima, the serene beach he is sitting on, and wonders if the evening will come soon. It's winter, but what sort of winter is this? Shouldn't it be colder?

Father and son pile up sand, creating mountains to decorate with shells and rocks they collected from the nearby forest. Every now and then, the father instinctively rubs the sand off his hands.

'Where's Mum?'

'With Hana, up that hill. There's another installation. Do you want to go?'

The child shakes his head, and Dr Fujita bends down to pick up another shell.

Someone told him about the Archives of Heartbeats months ago, and he, having wanted to take his family away for a while, waited for a weekend when he was sure he wouldn't have to work overtime and booked the flight.

His wife Yui asked him in a whisper if it was necessary to go so far. But he reassured her that they didn't even need to pack a suitcase: 'It's just two days, I'm curious to visit this place. We'll leave on Friday evening and return on Monday at dawn, so Hana and Yūto won't miss any school.'

The children were intrigued by the idea of listening to thousands of different people's heartbeats, but what really excited them was the idea of going on a trip: that hard-to-describe feeling of imagining themselves climbing onto a plane, boarding a ferry and sleeping in a hotel room.

As he expected, Yūto, the younger of the two, was distracted at the Teshima museum. The sun was calling him outside; after visiting only the first room of the Archive, he tugged at the sleeve of his father's coat and said he wanted to go: 'I don't understand it, I'm bored.'

In recent years, Dr Fujita has been seeing what his son is truly like: impatient and extremely sensitive, he throws terrifying tantrums when he's not well, hurls things around and responds to any kind of reproach with 'So are you!' Where has the child gone who used to beg to be picked up, then throw his head back and roar with laughter; who would snuggle up when his father read picture books to him by torchlight before bed?

'Let him go, Takeshi,' his wife whispered in his ear. 'Just make him promise to come back to record his heartbeat. I'll go with him, don't worry.'

Dr Fujita watched them from the large window behind the listening station, a wide rectangle that looked out on precisely the spot Yūto had chosen, running away from the chasing waves.

While listening to the heartbeats of a dozen or so strangers, Dr Fujita was amused by the way he found himself identifying anomalies here and there, making diagnoses, distinguishing elderly hearts from young ones, and hearts that were in distress.

Once he had finished going round with Hana, his eldest daughter, he called his son and wife back in. They all recorded their heartbeats.

That was when Yui said she also wanted to visit the Whispering Forest, an installation created by the same artist on the hill next to Mount Danzan, about an hour's walk away.

'It's full of wind chimes.'

Hanging from each one was a strip of paper, like the *tanzaku* which were attached to bamboo branches during *Tanabata*, the Star Festival, on the night in July when wishes are granted.

'You can write the name of someone you love and let it sing forever in the wind,' added Hana, appearing behind Yui's shoulder.

She is still a little girl, but to her father, she has already lived a lifetime, completed it, and been born again. Now she is at the beginning of her second life. Some evenings, curled up on the sofa, Yui and

her husband agree that Hana may be the wisest creature in the family.

'We could write Sachiko's name and our grand-
mothers' names and Mum's name.'

When Hana says 'Mum', she means Dr Fujita's
first wife, Akiko, her biological mother, who passed
away many years ago. Sachiko is Yui's first daughter.
She was swept away in the Tōhoku tsunami in 2011.

Theirs is a second family, deeply attached to the
memory of the first and all the connections that
remain within people even after those they love have
passed away. Death, Hana sometimes says, doesn't
have to take someone away from you.

Since she was a child, Hana has loved everything
that celebrates the remembrance of the dead: candles
in Western churches, prayers during the Day of the
Dead, or the *Higan* rituals in Japan. She has discovered, over the years, the strength that comes from
writing and posting letters with no recipient, or travelling to the Wind Phone in Iwate and making long
phone calls to her mother.

'Of course, go ahead. I don't think Yūto will
manage – he'll get tired and you won't enjoy it as

much. I'll stay here on the beach with him,' says Dr Fujita. 'Let's meet back at the hotel later, take your time.'

An hour later, Yui and Hana are in the Whispering Forest, holding each other tight. All around them, chimes tinkle gently and the wind whispers names. They read some of the strips of paper, and write some of their own. The sky gradually changes colour.

They stay until the caretaker tells them it's almost closing time. Then they make their way down to the hotel, which is a short distance from the port.

They hold hands; they're not sad. They might seem so to strangers when they learn about all they have lost, but they are at peace. So is Dr Fujita, who rarely talks about his personal life. For them, their departed loved ones are a place they keep going back to, and nostalgia is a feeling they know well. It's like huddling in front of a fire after a downpour and waiting to dry off completely, knowing that a small patch will remain damp forever.

chapter one

SHŪICHI WAS RESTLESS. NO MATTER what he did, he longed to be doing something else; wherever he was, he would have preferred to be elsewhere.

Always torn between fiction and reality, he immersed himself in the pages of his books with the sole purpose of disappearing. He projected himself completely into the landscapes he drew, making them ever more intricate as he imagined hiding in the undergrowth, or curling up in a neglected corner of a house. He attached handles to the walls, imagining secret passages between rooms. No one, not even the most attentive reader, would have been able to find them.

Shūichi thought about Kenta and wondered what he was doing, what he was having for tea, whether he was practising his *kanji*.

He missed him and knew that Sayaka was right: he needed to open up a way back, to face things. Especially because, while he was waiting, those things were changing.

'How do you catch a boy-fish? How do you convince him to come back?'

When he finally made up his mind, Shūichi set aside all his work: he declined a magazine cover, pushed back the delivery of a poster, and put off responding to the organisers of the annual exhibition. It took three days, during which time he forgot to take the bins out or change into pyjamas to sleep. Every so often, he would wander into the kitchen, drink a glass of orange juice and grab a handful of chocolates from the drawer.

One evening, having not heard from him for a few days, Sayaka climbed the hill and headed towards his house. She pushed open the gate, went into the garden, and stopped outside the living-room window.

A bubble of light floated out from inside, and there was Shūichi in the middle of it, hunched over the table, engrossed in his drawing. The light had returned to his face too, shining in his eyes as they stared at the paper.

If anyone had ever asked her, Sayaka would have said that it was Shūichi's mysterious concentration that had made her fall in love with him. He looked as though he was holding his breath as he lived, as if he existed only in suspended animation. Shūichi spoke, walked and laughed, yet a part of him wasn't there. He was elsewhere, in a place in his mind that only he knew.

Without knocking on the door, Sayaka took a series of small steps backwards until she was at the gate and then on the street. She looked up and saw that the evening had disappeared. She observed, without hurry, the clusters of stars that had appeared in the night sky.

She wandered through the Concubine's Tunnel and down the opposite side of the mountain.

During those days, Shūichi went through Kenta's schoolbooks. For each character that he had to learn

259

by the end of the year, Shūichi created a drawing and a story. He made seven flip books, each containing ten *kanji*; each ideogram first forming then dissolving between the pages as they were flipped. He also sketched a small cat in the top right-hand corner, which ran alongside the *kanji*, stopping every so often to lick its paw, or yawn.

He loved making them so much, and wondered why no one had thought of it before.

He packaged them up in home-made gift wrap and, the following afternoon, headed down to the Tōshoji Bridge and sat on a bench in the small park next to it, which had recently been renovated. In recent months, Shūichi and Kenta had watched the construction work with curiosity: they had witnessed the inspection of the experts with their rulers, plans and white helmets; they had studied the evolution of the fences, the replacement of the benches. They had also seen a cat take residence in the stump of a dead tree, and since then, they had nicknamed it 'Cat Stump Park'.

When Shūichi spotted Kenta on the bridge at exactly two o'clock, his feet dragging behind him and his school bag resembling a huge shell on his back, he was startled. He looked taller. Shūichi stood up and, before the boy could react, handed him the package with a confident smile.

In the following days, Shūichi intentionally under-took other actions to bring them closer together again. He intercepted Kenta on his way to school to let him know it was going to rain later on; he left the latest Pokémon encyclopaedia, which he'd got an advance copy of from an editor friend, on the steps of his house.

He followed Sayaka's advice, which was mainly to express his care for the child. Even though some-thing had changed for Kenta, it was important for him to see that Shūichi's door was still open.

Sometimes, Aya's horrified face when he admitted he didn't understand his life bounced around in Shūichi's mind. But – he had thought at the time – trying to understand was overrated. To make a day meaningful, you had to come up with a need for a particular type of paper, a whim for an out-of-season fruit, something that was difficult to obtain. Without needs, the days were endless.

Shūichi was astonished to realise that, compared to

two years ago, he was less afraid of suffering. He could now somehow see that love – the kind that worked – mattered most when it came from yourself.

'It is loving, not being loved, that counts.'

Thanks to this sentence, which his mother often repeated when he was a child and for some reason had suddenly floated back into his mind, he was finally convinced that a good childhood was to be loved to such an extent and in such blessed abundance that you could afford, one day, to be the one who loves.

Then, one evening, Shūichi received a call at home from an unfamiliar number. It was eight o'clock.

'Good evening, Maeda-san. It's Kenta's mother.'

'Oh, good evening, how are you?'

'Unfortunately, it's a tricky time . . .'

Without beating around the bush, Mrs Ogawa explained to him that her mother-in-law, who lived in Fukushima, had had a heart attack and that she and her husband needed to go up there immediately. Apart from them, the elderly woman didn't really have anyone else. From her tense and tired voice, Shūichi sensed that the woman would have preferred to avoid the burden.

'Can I help in any way?'

'It's very kind of you to ask.'

'Do you want me to take care of Kenta until you come back? That way, he won't have to miss school . . . I'd be more than happy to.'

'Oh thank you, I can't express the relief I feel right now. That's exactly what I wanted to ask you. It's impossible to reach Kamakura Family Support at this hour, and with such short notice it would be difficult to get someone's help. My son doesn't have any close friends at school, unfortunately, else I would have avoided bothering you . . .'

'It's no bother, really.'

'By the way, Mrs Ōno did have Kenta to stay in the past,' the woman said, her voice sounding more relaxed. 'He's comforted by the familiarity of the house.'

Shūichi was surprised but didn't say anything.

'You see, Maeda-san, I don't think Kenta likes the lady from the organisation very much, the one who looked after him when he was poorly in the winter,' she chuckled. 'I think he might have played some rather unpleasant pranks on her in the past, and the poor woman is at the end of her tether.'

Shūichi laughed along with her. Kenta had told

him about the mischief he got up to with his babysitters. The cruellest, in Shūichi's opinion, was removing the last three pages of a thriller one of them was reading; the most innocent was hiding one's shoes so well that she had to borrow a pair of slippers to go home in. He remembered witnessing a conversation on the street with one of the ladies who used to look after him: in a slow, high-pitched voice the elderly woman bent down and asked the child: 'Do you know what my name is?' and Kenta replied earnestly: 'Have you forgotten your own name?'

That aspect of Kenta's character had surprised Shūichi at first, then amused him. The thing that had most stuck with him was the serious expression on Kenta's face when Shūichi had asked him the reason for his evident antipathy, and he had replied, 'Because they pretend to love me, but they don't really care about me at all.'

In Shūichi's mind, that was the moment when the timid and fearful creature that Kenta had first seemed finally shook off all its generality to become the precise eight-year-old in front of him: the one who stole from his garage; chose any sweets that had strawberries on the packet; the troublesome, wounded, even vulgar one who he had learned to love. Of the generic 'boy', nothing remained.

'Do you need me to come and pick him up or will you drop him off?' Shūichi asked.

'We'll come in the car in about an hour, if that works for you.'

'Perfect, I'll get his room ready.'

When the conversation ended, Shūichi didn't go straight to make Kenta's bed, but walked down the corridor heading for his own room. Accompanied by the rapid and cheerful beating of his heart, he took out the family photographs. They needed dusting off, a couple of them needed replacing, and he considered the most suitable placement for them.

Shūichi had stumbled upon them a few days earlier, wrapped in a cloth and tucked under his mother's bed. Naively, in her confused way of dealing with sorrow, she had hidden them so that when her son came to visit he wouldn't suffer upon seeing the photos of Shingo.

Shūichi had brought them to his own room, determined to return them to their rightful positions in the house. He didn't admit it to himself because he still feared its fragility, but this courage was largely thanks to the developments of the past few months: the friendship of Kenta, the company of Sayaka, and the unexpected lightness that seemed to have returned to his life.

He would arrange them in the living room, prominently displayed.

'Not just yet, but soon,' he told himself, and gently stroked his fingertip along the faces of Shingo, his mother and father, his grandfather changed by the war, Aya, and finally his own childhood self.

Shūichi took off his overalls, pulled on a pair of jeans and a T-shirt, and found some fresh sheets and towels in the wardrobe. He went to make Kenta's bed.

*The page from The Pillow Book by Sei Shōnagon
that Sayaka opened by chance the evening she
had seen Shūichi through the window*

29

Things that make one's heart beat faster

- Sparrows feeding their young
- To pass a place where babies are playing
- To sleep in a room where fine incense has been burned
- To notice that one's elegant Chinese mirror has become a little cloudy
- To see a gentleman stop his carriage before one's gate and instruct his attendants to announce his arrival
- To wash one's hair, make one's toilet, and put on scented robes; even if not a soul sees one, these preparations still produce an inner pleasure

- It is night and one is expecting a visitor. Suddenly one is startled by the sound of raindrops, which the wind blows against the shutters

'How's it going?' Shūichi asked Kenta as soon as they got into the house.

Mrs Ogawa had hugged her son tight at the door and waved goodbye emotionally from the car as it pulled away.

'Fine.'

'I'm sorry to hear about your grandma, I hope she gets better soon.'

'Grandma's old . . . but she's strong.'

'That's important. Are you hungry?'

'A bit.'

'Do you want to do something before dinner?'

'Like what?'

'We've got the whole collection of Studio Ghibli films.'

'I know.'

'Did you watch them with Mrs Ōno?'

'Sometimes, when she was feeling nostalgic.'

'Nostalgic for what?'

'For when there were children in the house.'

'She said that?'

'She said that.'

The first evening Kenta stayed with him, Shūichi refrained from asking any questions, not wanting to put any pressure on the boy. They had dinner and watched a film from the collection. Shūichi filled the bathtub with hot water, but Kenta wanted to take a shower. When he put him to bed, Shūichi asked if he wanted him to read something. Kenta nodded, so Shūichi went down to the living room to get a volume of fairy tales, but when he returned, Kenta was already fast asleep.

The next morning, Shūichi made breakfast, helped Kenta pack his bag for school, and walked him part of the way down from the Concubine's Tunnel so that he wouldn't have to go past the cemetery on his own. He didn't say anything, just made a generic excuse about an errand he had to run in the Hase neighbourhood, but he smiled when he noticed that Kenta was no longer afraid of the graves. Childhood was slowly receding.

Shūichi remembered the emotion he felt at times with Shingo, the idea that just when he thought he had finally got a grasp on who he was, the child would change again. No matter how hard you tried, it was impossible to ever understand someone in their entirety.

After two days, Shūichi and Kenta seemed to have returned to their old routines: afternoon tea, studying *kanji* and arithmetic, telling fantastical stories, sharing their love of insects. The only additions were the dinners and the evenings. They invited Sayaka for dinner a couple of times and played charades and cards until late.

One evening, passing by Shūichi's desk, Kenta peeked at the drawings he was working on and noticed that something was different. He saw colour, waves of sunshine yellow and peony red, a green so vivid it was almost shouting.

'Do you want to have the first bath?' Shūichi called from the hallway, and Kenta jumped. Motionless, in the steadiest voice he could muster, he replied that he would rather go in after.

The child waited until the man had closed the door behind him and resumed flipping through the pages. There were so many delicately drawn scenes, and he was astounded by the sea of life that floated within each one: fish, jellyfish, leaves inhabited by unusual insects, snails with disproportionately long antennae emerging from bushes. Kenta thought that these drawings looked nothing like the books – which were of course brilliant – Mrs Ōno had proudly shown him. He would never admit it to Shūichi, partly out of shyness and partly embarrassment, but there was something new about these illustrations, and so beautiful that just looking at them made him feel happy.

Meanwhile, Kenta's parents, reassured by his lively voice on the phone and his grandmother's improved condition, decided to stay a few more days in Fukushima. They told their son about their walks back and forth from home to the supermarket or from home to the hospital, and the surprise they had experienced at mundane things: the local specialities in the refrigerator aisle, the thick dialect of the locals that they struggled to understand, his father's child-hood memories, and chance encounters with old schoolmates and retired teachers. This forced vacation seemed to be doing them good too, to the extent that Shūichi wondered if their marital crisis was the result of an ungluing of their lives rather than a lack of love. In that case, it could be repaired. He shared this thought with Kenta the following day when the child, clumsily attempting to conceal his own hopes, asked him.

On Sunday, they decided to do extraordinary things. For lunch, they ordered curry delivered to the house and added all the optional extras: cheese baked in a wafer, crab croquettes, grilled vegetables, hard-boiled eggs and fried onion rings. They also planned to watch all the episodes of *Detective Conan* in a marathon that would start in the morning and, with a few breaks, finish at night.

In those days of perfect harmony, Shūichi tried to convince himself that the mysterious gloominess that had silenced Kenta for the past two months and caused the child to avoid him on the street hadn't happened.

Certain things come and go; perhaps it wasn't even that something had happened, but just a change of feeling that Kenta himself wasn't even aware of. Life behaves in strange ways.

In the evening, as the television continued to fill the living room with its multicoloured glow, Shūichi told Kenta to sit down, as dinner was almost ready.

He went to fetch the bowls with the potato salad and tempura. He had been busy in the kitchen while Kenta continued watching Conan; he wanted to surprise him. It was their final night together as Kenta's parents would be returning from Fukushima the next day.

As Shūichi entered the living room and walked towards the dining table, Kenta was standing in front of the photographs. That afternoon, waiting for the potatoes to boil, he had finished arranging the frames and placed them in the living room near the window.

'That's Shingo,' Shūichi said, noticing that Kenta was standing still in front of the picture of him, 'my son.'

He placed the dishes in the middle of the table. He was satisfied with the result.

But when he approached Kenta, he noticed that the child was crying.

'What's wrong? Why are you upset?' he asked, alarmed.

Kenta pulled his hand out of his left pocket and clenched his fist tightly.

'Kenta?'

'His lucky charm . . .' the child stammered.

'Lucky charm?'

He cried even louder.

'What are you saying, Kenta? I don't understand.'

'His lucky charm, I . . .'

The child turned suddenly and buried his face in Shūichi's shirt.

Shūichi looked down and saw Kenta's dark head, the exact same height as Shingo's the last time he had hugged him after an argument with Aya: their son wanted a dog, or a fish, or a flying deer! But his mother, strangely decisive, had replied that she couldn't have any more living things in the house.

'Kenta, can you explain what happened?'

Shūichi crouched down to his height and the child threw himself into his arms. The man held him tight, as if telling him that he was there, holding up the world.

They remained in a tight embrace for several minutes. Then Kenta slowly moved away, rubbing his sleeve across his snot- and tear-streaked face, and opened his fist.

Shūichi saw a thread, but he didn't immediately understand what it was. Only when he picked it up between his fingers and examined it closely did he recognise it.

The scene was cut at that moment. Years later, Shūichi would have forgotten entirely about the dinner, the television where Conan's adventures continued to unfold. There would only be the child next to him, the thread of fabric, and a light so intense that everything else looked bleached.

It was the bracelet he had given to Shingo in elementary school when his son was still afraid of water. On the day of his first swimming lesson, Shūichi had assured him that if he tied it around his wrist, nothing bad could happen: the bracelet was a powerful talisman.

Shūichi looked at Kenta, surprised. How had that object ended up in his hands?

The child, still shaken by sobs, did not lift his eyes

from the palm of his hand, which, although empty now, he continued to hold out towards Shūichi.

'I stole it,' he repeated desperately. 'It's my fault that he lost his luck.'

doki doki

'I had a horrible dream last night.'

'What happened?'

'My mum left my dad, got married to someone else and took me away.'

The older boy sat in silence. He picked up an acorn, cracked it between his thumb and index finger, and tossed it down the hill. Then he asked, 'Are they still arguing?'

'They're always arguing . . . I hate it when they argue.'

The older boy nodded. He liked the autumn; his father said it was the season when everything important happened.

'Do your parents never argue?' the younger boy asked.

'No, never. But I don't know if they really love each other.'

'Why?'

'They seem sad together. Whenever I'm not there, they avoid being alone.'

'But they don't shout or say nasty things to each other.'

'No, they don't do that.'

The younger boy pulled a stone out of his pocket and hurled it over the metal fence to their left. The older boy's grandmother had once explained that those fences were there to protect them from the mountain, so if anything crumbled away at the top and tumbled down onto the road, it would be caught by the netting.

'Anyway, in the dream I couldn't find my way home. I didn't know where I was. I was alone and couldn't see anything, like being out at sea in the dark.'

'It sounds horrible . . .'

'Really horrible.'

'Whenever I have nightmares, I'm also always alone. I don't know where I am any more, and I'm convinced I'll never know again.'

The younger boy felt less sad. His friend also had nightmares and got scared. Maybe he even wet the bed sometimes too.

'Last week, the police came into school for road safety day. They said that every year in Japan hundreds of children go missing . . .'

The older boy burst in: 'My dad told me that too!'

'The police told us that some children run away because they're unhappy, but many are taken away, and no one hears anything from them ever again.'

'Nothing.'

'Nothing, forever.'

'Forever . . .'

'Yes, forever. It's like falling into a black hole and never getting out. I was happy to be allowed to walk to school on my own at first, but then I got scared. I don't know how it is in Tōkyō. This is a small town, but you get crazy people everywhere. So in year one I didn't want to go to school and home again on my own.'

The younger boy didn't say it, but some of his classmates teased him, and it really hurt when they called him a chicken.

The older boy, unaware of this, smiled. He stood up, still holding a handful of acorns.

'My mum says she doesn't care what others think,

and that it's better to be safe than sorry, so she walks with me. Sometimes my dad comes instead and tells me loads of stuff on the way. Then I go in and he goes to work.'

'Your dad writes books, right?'

'He draws them, and while he's drawing them, Bam! The story arrives.'

'Bam?'

'Yes, that's what he says: he draws, and then Bam! The story comes to life.'

Some emotions can only be experienced unconsciously.

After the first time, which defines their nature forever, feelings are never replicated with the same intensity again. Not because the people we meet later in life are less important, but because the structure of our emotions hardens, and is no longer open to transformation in that same reckless, definitive way.

Shūichi had thought about it when Shingo was born. That this child's soul would grow, and he would have all the space of the world in his life. The undefined acceptance that the child granted him was almost frightening. Whether it was a bicycle, a pile of scrap metal, or a sculpture worth millions of yen at auction, the plant that was this child would grow intertwined with Shūichi and Aya, with the substance that was their family. From a delicate sapling, Shingo would thicken out until he became bark, and his trunk would mould itself over time to accommodate the bicycle, the scrap metal, or the precious sculpture. He had no choice; it would all become a part of him.

It wasn't like that for adults, though. A fully grown plant would never accept that kind of alteration.

And yet for months, Shūichi had been thinking about Kenta with an intensity that, rather than settling, grew. He couldn't separate the boy from himself.

One morning in March, he woke up full of doubt that the love he felt for Shingo had been redirected towards Kenta. He imagined it as a miraculous grafting: a dormant bud fused onto an old branch, and the imprecise cut that, by a remarkable coincidence, turned out to be exactly right. Shūichi saw himself tightly wrapping the tape around it to ensure a successful graft.

How else could he explain the lightness he felt? Kenta sprouted up in his day, and blossomed in his memory. In the last two years, this had been the closest thing to joy.

When he had first seen Kenta, the resemblance

283

seemed so accurate he thought it was a product of his imagination. It wasn't so much his facial features, but his gestures, his use of certain expressions, his strange stutter that kept restarting a word from the beginning until it came out perfect.

He was certain he had never met him before, and yet he felt a sense of familiarity in Kenta, in everything he said, in the way he moved.

That was precisely what made it difficult. It hurt to talk to him, the way it hurts to think of things you love with such passion and conviction that it's impossible to admit they could one day cease to exist. But Shūichi had immediately understood that this was also an opportunity; perhaps the only one life would offer him.

So, as the days and weeks passed, Shūichi had gradually allowed Kenta into his heart. It was like falling into step with someone. Calibrating his speed, his stride, reaching out a hand and every time, on his right or left, finding another.

In the afternoons they spent together after school, Shūichi watched Kenta hunched over his books in the living room, running excitedly down the aisles of the supermarket, silhouetted on the streets of this city he so loved. Sometimes his heart ached so much he had to place a palm on his chest to calm it.

Observing Kenta, talking to him, giving him snacks, even scolding him, brought back memories of Shūichi's previous life. Reading the encyclopaedia with Kenta ushered in memories of Shingo. It was as if the two children were holding hands in his mind. When Shingo was passionate about something, he poured it into his own vocabulary. If it was insects, suddenly everything was about *exoskeletons, reproduction, biological cycles,* and *environmental adaptation*; if he had fallen in love with Ancient Egypt, the world around him revealed only *hieroglyphics, dynasties, mummies,* and *pharaohs*. The same thing happened with Kenta.

Every evening since he was five, Shingo recounted his day to his father, and Shūichi, listening, would sketch it. Apart from the two of them, no one knew the secret of that hour spent together. Aya thought they were checking his homework or that Shūichi was trying to teach him something, so before leaving them alone, she would bring the child a cup of hot chocolate to make it feel like less of an ordeal.

Over the years, father and son had accumulated

a substantial stack of paper: the child providing the words, the adult giving them form and colour.

'One day we'll publish a book, the two of us, and we'll travel the world doing interviews and presentations,' Shūichi said one autumn evening.

'Even to Mars!' Shingo had added.

The following summer, he drowned in the swimming pool.

With the same secrecy as those slivers of night when father and son shared their adventures in hushed voices, on the day of the funeral, Shūichi slipped the stack of paper into the small coffin, at Shingo's side. He did it once everyone was heading back to the minibus, a moment before the box in which he lay would be closed and burned. Just the time it took for a hug, before the skin of his tiny son would vanish along with the paper.

The quote Shūichi wrote in his notebook on 16 August the previous year

'Failing to fetch me at first keep encouraged
Missing me one place search another
I stop somewhere waiting for you.'

—WALT WHITMAN, *LEAVES OF GRASS*

'Did my mother give you this bracelet? Mrs Ōno?' Shūichi asked Kenta gently.

Eventually, Kenta lowered his hand, but his eyes remained on the ground.

'Kenta, I'm glad it's you who has it,' Shūichi whispered to reassure him.

It was at that moment, as the sunset seeped into the room and Shūichi got up to turn on the lamp by the window, that an image flashed into his mind.

He saw two children at sunset, playing with a ball inside the Concubine's Tunnel. They were throwing it as far as possible, from one end of the tunnel to the other. It rolled along and they kicked it. One was Shingo. But who was the other? Could it have been Kenta? In those days, three years ago, Shūichi was absent, busy with an exhibition and rushing to finish the volume he was working on; he demanded

288

silence at home, and no one, not even Shingo, dared disturb him. Shūichi had taken him to Kamakura: Shingo loved staying at his grandmother's house and adored his father, holding no grudges against him for those moments of absorption that preceded the completion of a volume. He couldn't wait for Shūichi to finish his work and come back home full of stories to tell, with the freshly printed copy in his hands.

Shūichi looked at Kenta and smiled. 'You knew my son, didn't you? You used to play together when he came to visit his grandmother?'

Something about that memory moved him. It revealed the foresight of memory, which, without us noticing, records life and presents it to us when we are finally able to understand it.

The child playing with Shingo in the setting sun had to have been Kenta!

'Kenta, did you know Shingo?'

Kenta searched for an image in his mind that could calm him. Jumping from the desert island to his *kanji* book, he stopped at his science exercise book, where he had drawn a beetle so accurately that his teacher had given him a double stamp that read 'Well done!' with a star next to it.

'Kenta?'

'He was my best friend.'

Shūichi took the boy's hand and pulled him to sit on the couch.

'But I don't think I was his . . . Shingo was too good for me. He probably thought I was an idiot.'

'Why do you say that? I am sure you were a precious friend to him.'

Kenta wiped his sleeve across his face again. The fabric shimmered, as if a snail had crawled over it.

'Our birthday is on the same day.'

'Yours and Shingo's? Really?' Shūichi exclaimed with a laugh.

'The seventeenth of June, but I was born two years after him,' Kenta whispered and returned the smile.

'So you were also born during the rainy season . . . Shingo didn't like the rain. His mother and I did everything we could to make him love it.'

'I don't mind the rain.'

'Did my mother know? About the seventeenth of June?'

Kenta nodded.

Kenta had loved Shingo so much that he had tried to absorb even his mannerisms, the way his friend would push his hair back, the way he clicked his lips when he was annoyed, how his gestures expanded as he became more impassioned. It was unconscious at first, but then it became intentional, and the more he learned to imitate him, the stronger he felt.

That's why one afternoon when Shingo realised he had lost his bracelet on the beach and was frantically searching for it, repeating, 'My dad gave it to me, it's the most powerful lucky charm in the world,' Kenta helped him. They sifted through the sand until it was too dark.

They walked home, disheartened, but Shingo couldn't accept it. He kept telling Kenta how special that bracelet was: it was all thanks to the bracelet that he had learned to swim, and that he had ridden a horse when he was six and hadn't fallen off. Once, he had even won a toy at Luna Park, and he always found all the baseball balls when they played in the garden. 'All of them, every single time!' he exclaimed. Then he stopped talking as, step by step, the sadness crystallised. Kenta remained silent and walked beside him to his grandma's house. For the first time since they had been friends, Shingo entered the house without turning to wave goodbye.

Kenta never doubted the power of the amulet, and as he ran back down the hill to avoid spending too long near the cemetery, he worried that Shingo was annoyed with him. Perhaps he held him responsible for the incident. After all, they were playing together when he lost it, and if they hadn't gone to the beach, if he hadn't insisted on building the marble track, the bracelet would probably still be on Shingo's wrist. That's why he didn't turn to wave! He was angry!

The thought bothered Kenta so much that he told his parents he wasn't hungry, had a shower and went to bed. He couldn't sleep, tossing and turning nervously, until he decided that he would go back down to the beach as soon as the sun came up: he swore he would find the bracelet.

He woke up at dawn and left the house with a rake and a bucket. He scoured the stretch of beach for hours while children all around him dug holes, caught crabs and looked for shells, chased each other, and plunged into the sea.

When he had to give up because it was lunchtime,

he headed back through the Concubine's Tunnel. He was desperate, determined to apologise to his friend until he forgave him. His face was streaked with tears, and his back burned from the sun.

That was when he found Shingo's bracelet.

It was lying on the street, not far from Shingo's grandmother's gate. It must have fallen off in the morning before they went down to the beach.

Kenta picked the bracelet up and the joy was so overwhelming that at first he didn't know what to do with it. The bracelet was dirty, as if a car had run over it, and the bright red thread was covered in mud stains.

It was tempting to return it to Shingo immediately, but Kenta thought that washing the bracelet and returning it to him in the best possible condition would make him more of a hero in his friend's eyes. He rushed home and cleaned it, drying it carefully with a hairdryer. He waited, savouring every second that separated him from the moment he could say to Shingo, 'Here it is, I found it!'

After lunch, he climbed up the hill and knocked on the door. Where was Shingo? Mrs Ōno said her grandson had left for Tōkyō that morning and wouldn't be back in Kamakura for another three or four weeks. Did he want her to pass a message on?

Kenta was initially disappointed, and he cried in frustration. Then he thought that, in Shingo's absence, he could test the power of the lucky charm.

On Monday, he wore the bracelet for his running race, and he finished third, which had never happened before.

On Wednesday, he wore it for his Japanese exam; he rubbed it with his right fingertip, and, magically, the exact succession of *kanji* came to mind. He guessed − knowing he hadn't studied it − the strokes of a character that he vaguely remembered from the textbook. Once again, the bracelet worked.

He put it away in a drawer for two weeks, then slipped it onto his wrist the evening his father came home late from work. His mother was waiting for him so she could go out with her friends from high school, and usually in that kind of situation they argued so loudly and for so long that Kenta would have to pull the covers over his head and press his palms against his ears to drown it out. But that evening, two of her four friends had the flu and the dinner was postponed.

Having witnessed yet another miracle, Kenta had no doubt about the power of the lucky charm. He felt a bit guilty towards Shingo, but he thought his friend would have been more than happy to share some of his luck with him.

Usually, when Shingo came to visit his grand-mother in Kamakura, he wouldn't go and call on Kenta to play, but somehow the two boys always ended up meeting in the streets of the town. In reality, on Saturdays and Sundays, Kenta would go up the mountain on purpose, through the Concubine's Tunnel, and look for signs of his friend's presence: a bicycle in the garden, toys on the path, the scent of the cakes and pastries that the old lady only baked when her grandson was coming.

But now he was fearful of having to give the bracelet back, Kenta began to avoid the area on weekends. He would stay at home on Saturdays or go shopping with his parents in Ōfuna or Fujisawa. He felt like a coward, a bad person, even, but his parents had been getting along lately and Kenta was convinced it was all thanks to the bracelet. He never took it off his wrist any more.

After another three weeks, during which his parents had gradually started arguing again, and the holiday they were supposed to go on in August for the Festival of the Dead fell through, Kenta realised that his luck was fading and it was probably because he had been dishonest. He missed Shingo, and he was haunted by the memory of his friend's sadness as he repeated how important the bracelet was to him on their way home from the beach. The guilt he felt had ruined everything.

Then, one Saturday, Kenta mustered up the courage to run up the hill to Shingo's grandmother's, arriving at her door panting. He rang the bell, determined to give the bracelet back. He would hand it over to her, and she would find a way to get it to her grandson.

However, when the woman explained to him – her eyes swollen with tears – what had happened to Shingo, Kenta couldn't move. He didn't really understand. Even once he was home, he still couldn't comprehend what she had said. He had lunch, dinner, went to bed, and continued not understanding.

The idea started appearing in different places: his mother, a week later, talking about the tragedy at the dinner table (she had heard it from a neighbour); a cartoon on TV where the protagonist fell into the sea during a storm; the strange sensation he could sense in the air when the bracelet was present in the room.

It became definitively clear when all his happiness vanished.

Doki doki went Kenta's heart when he was with Shin-go. *Doki doki*, it was the soundtrack of their every conversation. It beat and beat, his heart beat so strongly: *doki doki*, *doki doki*.

Shingo, who had taught him how to catch crabs with his bare hands, that if you write things down, they stay with you forever, that true happiness happens when you do more with less; he, in his earnest and arrogant way, had taught him about friendship, and through friendship, love.

Kenta had felt so proud that his friend, who lived in the capital city – in Tōkyō! – wanted to die there in Kamakura, right where he was born. He liked it when Shingo placed his hand on his shoulder when they started playing football, a greeting someone had probably taught him and that he was now passing on to Kenta. He felt chosen.

Someone once wrote that we end up resembling our ideal self, that 'the face we are born with, little by little, is superseded by the face we desire.' Kenta was convinced he was starting to resemble that boy who was exactly two years older. He had even started drawing the conversations he remembered, even in fragments, as Shingo had once suggested. He still remembered Shingo's joy when he explained how wonderful it was to be able to write. Finally things could be stopped!

Twenty years later, talking about it with his girlfriend, Kenta would give a name to what he had felt for the older boy. Other than for his mother and father, it was probably the first time he felt love.

What Aya and Shūichi did to try to make Shingo love the rain

- Aya bought him a Pikachu raincoat, an umbrella that changed colour when it got wet, and two boots with Pikachu's face on the toes.
- Shūichi gave him the *Dictionary of Words for Rain*. He managed to teach him thirty-six out of the twelve hundred words it contained.
- For every rainy day, Aya would put a coin in Shingo's capybara-shaped piggy bank. They called it 'The Rain Bank'.
- On their way home from nursery, Shūichi always allowed him, unconditionally, to jump in all the puddles, even the ones filled with mud, and deep enough to soak him down to his underwear. Then, when they got home, he would quickly put the boy under the shower and hand-wash the clothes so that Aya never found out.

chapter
two

'IT'S MY FAULT . . . the charm.'

The words wouldn't come out.

'Kenta, do you think Shingo drowned because he didn't have the lucky bracelet on his wrist?'

'I don't know, maybe.'

'Shingo had it on that day.'

Kenta looked up, bewildered.

'That's impossible, I had it!'

Shūichi smiled. He felt the kind of deep happiness you feel when you've organised a wonderful surprise for someone and you're anticipating the joy on their face. 'Shingo had replaced that bracelet three times already, and the last time was just two months before that day.'

Kenta signalled that he didn't understand.

'Shingo always had it on his wrist, but it wasn't the same one. I replaced it several times during the two years he had it. Didn't you know?'

Kenta shook his head.

'Shingo's grandmother, Mrs Ōno, taught me as a child that when we really love something and believe it has magic inside it, it's best to buy more than one. That way, if it gets old or lost or broken, we have a spare,' Shūichi said. 'Ever since I was a little boy, my mother bought at least two of everything: I have three copies of my favourite books, multiple identical scarves and gloves; this house is full of matching plates, clothes, lamps, accessories . . . haven't you noticed?'

Laughing, Shūichi pointed out all the duplicates in the living room and kitchen, an abundance of things, objects, ingredients. If there was going to be a battle against wear and tear, forgetfulness, and mundane accidents, Mrs Ōno was winning before it even started.

Holding Kenta's little hand tight in his, Shūichi went up the stairs, opened wardrobes and drawers, and told him about his mother and her obsession with happiness. He told anecdotes, like the bicycle accident when he was five and the cat that disappeared in the earthquake, explaining it to the child with the transparent language you use when you no longer want to keep anything hidden. He couldn't help but laugh at all the lies the woman had made up to protect him from pain. The tenderness he felt towards her grew, and for the first time, Shūichi felt his mother's legacy in his heart: a time in his life when he had been happy, in a wonderful and ridiculous way.

Still holding his hand, Shūichi led Kenta back down to the living room. He continued the conversation because he knew that while magical thinking in childhood carries extraordinary powers, it also comes with guilt, and Kenta must have truly believed he was responsible in some way for Shingo's death. He wanted to give him a hug, but he didn't. What Kenta needed right now was the truth.

'You know, after his first swimming lesson went well and Shingo came back from school excited, saying it was all thanks to the bracelet, the lucky charm, I went back to the shop and bought twenty more. Yes, twenty! Enough to last him through high school, considering how often he lost them,' Shūichi continued, laughing. 'If he seemed sad that day, when he lost it, it was probably because he had promised me he would look after it so many times.'

Kenta didn't say anything, so Shūichi put his hands on his shoulders.

'He had it on his wrist that day too, Kenta,' he whispered, planting a small kiss on his head. 'It was not your fault.'

That night, after Kenta had cried twenty thousand leagues of tears and shared a hundred thousand memories of Shingo, Shūichi lay in bed, unable to fall asleep.

He thought of Shingo's red bracelet, the exact moment when he was six years old and he had tied it around his wrist for the first time, his hesitant yet hopeful face, the 100-yen shop where he had bought it, the day the shop closed, and how angry he got that everything was always changing in Tōkyō. He recalled Shingo whispering that he had lost it in

304

Kamakura, at the beach, and how sorry he was; he saw himself teasing him, telling him he'd lose an arm or an ear he was so careless! But Shingo didn't laugh that time, and it had dawned on Shūichi that his son was growing up because things didn't affect him in the same way any more.

How was it possible for memories to flood back like that? Shūichi wondered in the darkness of the room. It was like standing on unstable ground and, after a series of small landslides, half the mountain came down.

Feeling liberated from two hundred kilos of clutter, he thought that the beat of his heart was changing again.

He decided that the next day he would talk to Kenta's mother. He would tell her how much he cared for her son, how important he was in his life.

doki doki

'Go on then! Quiz me!'

'What's the biggest fish in the world?'

'Whale shark.'

'And the biggest animal?'

'Whale.'

'On land?'

'Elephant.'

'What's the biggest flower in the world?'

'Rafflesia . . . that's what Gloom is inspired by in Pokémon, the stinky flower.'

'And the biggest insect in the world?'

'The *Titanus giganteus.*'

'And the biggest child in the world?'

'The biggest man in the world when he was a child, isn't it?'

The summer passed peacefully.

The atmosphere at home relaxed a little, and Kenta's parents took him to Hokkaido, which had been his dream for a long time. Almost every day, Kenta sent Shūichi photos of the colourful stripes of Furano's flower fields, a dark dot on the other side of a river, which he explained was 'a huuuuuge brown bear' that he had spotted from the boat off the rugged coast of Shiretoko.

Shūichi responded with long comments, adding facts and curiosities about the places the child was visiting. When he was bored, especially on long bus or train rides, Kenta sent him riddles, pencil sketches of seals, salt marshes, and nonsensical voice notes that recorded the sound of the sea, the faint sound of whale song. It was a wonderful exercise of the imagination for Shūichi.

Through those exchanges, Shūichi became closer to Kenta's mother too. One evening, when he called at the agreed time but the child was already asleep in the tent, Shūichi and Mrs Ogawa had a long conversation.

Shūichi finally found out her name (Naoko) and learned that Kenta's father had suffered a form of depression from working too much, but he had finally found a new job in July. He had given himself this holiday between the old job and the new one. With the holiday atmosphere and a few glasses too many, the woman confided in Shūichi that after years of conflict, things between them had started to get better. 'If you don't like your work, it eats away at your life and your relationships,' she said. 'Getting older helps too.'

Shūichi was happy that a solution was near. He was happy for the couple, but particularly for Kenta. The child needed to learn the kind of love that he could one day build a family on.

After ending the phone call with Mrs Ogawa, Shūichi phoned Aya.

In a few weeks, it would be 16 August – the day they visited their son's grave every year. Usually, they would exchange a handful of polite messages to agree on the time and exact location. But that evening, Shūichi felt the desire to call her and catch up on the three months that had passed since the last time they spoke.

'Hello, Aya.'

'Shūichi, is something wrong?'

'No, nothing. I just wanted to talk.'

He asked her how she was doing, told her about the child who had been rummaging around his house in the autumn: who Kenta was, his friendship with Shingo, and the bracelet. He also told her about Kenta's sense of guilt.

'There is no disaster that can be the responsibility of a child,' Aya commented with tenderness. 'It's the magical thinking of children; they feel capable of doing both grand and terrible things.'

'That's true,' Shūichi said. 'The whole universe rests in their tiny hands.' In that moment, he remembered that it was Aya he had first talked to about the superpowers Shingo believed he possessed.

During their long conversation, the calming words of the past resurfaced. Shūichi told her about all the changes he had made in his childhood home, and how Kenta had forced him to put everything back in its place. They laughed about the stubbornness of children, how they were reassured by familiarity and routine. Shūichi also confessed that he missed his mother: on warm evenings at dawn and at sunset, it seemed to him that her gentle ghost floated through the rooms.

'I loved your mother.'

'I know, and she knew it too.'

'And how's work? When is your next book coming out?'

Shūichi told her that the book, the one about a shipwrecked child, would be out in October.

'Don't send it to me this time. I want to go to the bookshop and buy it.'

Shūichi felt a pang of nostalgia and profound relief when Aya told him that she would soon qualify as a nursery-school teacher, that she folded complex *origami* in her free time (she had even invented some new ones), and that she had been seeing a man for a few months now and they were due to marry in winter.

Life goes on, thought Shūichi, and he congratulated her.

310

A few weeks later, it was 16 August. When they met at the gates of the cemetery, it felt like the continuation of the conversation they had started that evening.

Chatting away, they walked side by side along the path. They gave the gravestone a thorough clean, replaced the flowers and placed down their offerings. They remembered their disastrous first holiday in Odawara, when, even though they had booked three nights in a hotel, they hurried home early because of two-year-old Shingo's tantrums. Aya told him about the children she looked after at the kindergarten, how wonderful their energy was, and how afraid she'd been at first that being around them would sharpen the absence of her son.

'But now I see Shingo in fragments, in the gestures and features of each of those children. It's like a puzzle: each child provides me with a piece. Being with them makes me feel close to him.'

Aya took a paper fish out of her pocket, then a stingray and a whale shark, and placed them between the offerings.

'Did you make them?'

'Yes, I find folding paper very calming.'

'You've always been good at crafts, especially the

ones that require a lot of patience,' Shūichi said, recalling the elaborate sweets she used to prepare for Shingo's afternoon tea.

'You write books where children save themselves from the water, and I make *origami* fish that swim around happily.'

They headed towards the exit. Aya's partner was waiting in the car in front of the cemetery, and when Shūichi caught sight of him, he bowed in the man's direction. At first, he only saw part of his torso, but when he looked up, the man had got out of the car and was bowing back to him. Shūichi noticed how kind the expression on his face was.

'I'm happy for you,' he said to Aya and hugged her gently. 'Next year, invite your husband as well. He'll officially be part of the family by then.'

'Yes, and you introduce me to Kenta. I'd like to meet him.'

'Of course.'

Aya wiped a few small tears from her face.

'Oh, wait a minute,' she said, reaching into her handbag.

When she opened her palm, Shūichi saw something red. It was a paper heart.

Aya pressed her thumb and index finger behind the scarlet *origami*, and the heart started to pulsate.

'*Doki doki*,' she said softly and smiled.

'Is it for me?'

'Who else?'

As she got into the vehicle, Aya waved one last time.

When the car disappeared from view, Shūichi opened his palm and looked at the paper heart.

He gently held it from behind, as if cradling its delicate wings, and it started to beat again.

On the evening of 16 August, Shūichi texted Sayaka.

He didn't tell her how he had spent the day, as having experienced it with such intensity was enough, without the need to recount it. Instead, he invited her out to dinner. They ate a bowl of fresh fish and rice at a restaurant overlooking the ocean in Enoshima. They talked and laughed for a long time. It was almost midnight when they took a taxi back to his house.

The next morning, when Sayaka kissed him goodbye at the door before rushing off to work, Shūichi stepped aside to let her pass. But she stopped at the threshold.

'I'm so glad you've decided to go to Teshima. The museum must be really special. When do you go?'

'In September, maybe October. Are you sure you don't want to come with me?'

'Yes, I told you. Because of my job, I can't be away for more than twenty-four hours,' Sayaka replied.

Shūichi nodded. Sayaka walked away, happily waving at him from the garden path before rushing back and kissing him again.

Through the slightly open door, Shūichi saw autumn approaching, the light breaking the leaves of the mountain into a dozen shades of green, the Concubine's Tunnel exhaling the scent of moss and fresh air. The vibrant yellows, amber reds and browns would soon descend in tiny steps, evening out all the colours.

He knew, in that moment, that something important was about to happen in his life.

The quote Shūichi copied into his notebook on
16 August of that year, alongside a sketch of a
scorpion and a stag beetle

'There is never much to say on happy days,'
added the Sphinx after a long silence, 'happiness
hates words.'

—FRIEDRICH DÜRRENMATT,
DAS STERBEN DER PYTHIA

The island of heartbeats

THERE IS A LIFE THAT is real and then there's a bundle of imaginary lives that branch out from it.

If there is one thing a child lives off, Shūichi thought, it is his imagination. A child grows up by imagining things that don't exist: monsters he cannot see; loves that draw him in; adventures he will never experience. It's not much different from what happens to an adult.

Proportionately, he thought, the life we dream is so much greater than the one we realise. So why do we give more value to reality than to our dreams?

They departed for Teshima on Friday afternoon.

The decision to bring Kenta with him was so obvious – and so sudden – that Shūichi was astonished he had been able to imagine going on the trip alone. Mr and Mrs Ogawa granted their son permission on the condition that they would only be away for a weekend and Kenta wouldn't miss any days of school.

The previous evening, they landed in Takamatsu from Haneda Airport. Kenta's parents had gone with them by train, on the Keikyū Line that departed from Yokohama.

Mrs Ogawa had stuffed Kenta's rucksack full of spare clothes and emergency medication. His father had given him his first camera as a gift. He had to temporarily confiscate it in the morning because, in his eagerness to photograph everything, the child was taking too long to leave the house.

They stayed in a hotel not far from Takamatsu-Chikkō Station and took the local train to visit the Konpira-san shrine, passing through a vast expanse of wheat fields.

They tackled the 1,368 steps of Konpira-san to reach an altitude of 421 metres. Caught off-guard by the rain, they had to shelter under a canopy for an hour. Then they hurried back to pick up their luggage from the hotel and boarded the ferry that, in half an hour, took them across to Teshima.

There weren't many people on board and Kenta, exhausted from their morning hike, fell asleep with the gentle swaying of the boat.

For the trip, they needed a rucksack that wasn't too heavy, plasters for if one of them fell over, and a flashlight to pierce the darkness.

As a child, Shūichi would open an atlas and long for the whole world. Not a specific place, but the sum of all the places drawn in pencil. He wasn't content with just a part of the map; he wanted it in its entirety.

That's what his mother used to tell him.

However, during their first real trip to Kyōto to visit his father's brother, Mrs Ōno noticed that her son didn't harbour a true curiosity for the world. Shūichi much preferred the tangled pile of coloured lines that depicted the universe in books.

'I remember your disappointment. Reality looked ugly; didn't live up to how you imagined it. That's when you started drawing.'

319

Kenta turned to Shūichi.

'Do things really look more beautiful when you draw them?'

'Apparently that's what I thought as a child. But now I'm not so sure.'

'For me, food is like that. I see the photo on the menu, but then when it's in front of me, it always seems smaller and less colourful.'

'And the taste?'

'It depends . . . I don't know that by looking at the menu.'

Getting off the ferry at Teshima, they took a bus – the only one that crossed the island from one side to the other – and then continued on foot.

It was autumn, but it felt like summer. Dragonflies fluttered around them and cicadas sang in the heat that would soon come to an end.

Kenta would occasionally stop to take a photo, quickly checking how it had come out on the screen, and, depending on his satisfaction, he would either take another or keep walking. Whenever he saw a big rock, a low wall or a bench, he would sit down to take notes in his notebook because he had promised his teacher he'd write a report on the trip.

The eastern slope of the hill was covered in green rice fields. Wandering along the paths and the few fishermen's houses, Kenta became talkative. He talked about school, the boys in his class, the girls in his class (he might have had a crush on one of them), and reminisced about Mrs Ōno. How wonderful it was to be near her. 'Tell me!' she would say each time they met, all silence and anticipation.

Suddenly, Kenta stopped.

'Do you hear it?' the child asked, looking at Shūichi. 'Do you hear it?'

The man stopped and listened. 'Not yet.'

It was after a few more steps that the air began to pulsate.

Shūichi crouched down to Kenta's level.

'We must be close.'

From the outside, the Archive looked like a forgotten piece of Lego on the beach. At least that's how it seemed to Shūichi.

Kenta, who still hadn't got used to the pulsating sound in the air, remained silent, alternating his gaze between the building and the sea.

The beach was white, and on the horizon you

could see the shapes of other islands floating untidily on the surface.

Shūichi called him and pushed open the door of the Archive. They found themselves in an extremely white room, where, behind a sort of counter, almost like a hospital reception, a man in his twenties welcomed them. He wore black-framed glasses, his hair was styled with gel, and he had on a white lab coat. He was the Archive attendant. Pinned to his chest was a name tag, with his first name and surname printed on it, but Shūichi wasn't paying attention to that.

They paid the entrance fee, and Kenta stuck close to Shūichi as the young man explained the route. In the background, they could hear the sound they had started to hear on the other side of the hill between the rice fields of Teshima.

'The "Heart Room" is behind this wall. What you hear is the sound of someone's heartbeat: a man, a woman, perhaps a child,' the young man said. 'The screen on the wall up there shows the number of heartbeats recorded so far from different parts of the world.' He lowered his finger and, as if reciting an ancient tale, recited a cluster of phrases he had read dozens of times in his room two years ago when he was still at university. 'We don't know the faces of these people. All we know is their names, surnames, and their location at the time of recording, some-times their age too, if they chose to provide it. Some of them may already be dead, and yet the beat of their heart continues to echo here on this small island in Japan.'

The young man placed the brochure on the counter and opened it to show them the route.

'Through that door, you enter the Heart Room, which is the centrepiece of the museum. It's dark, so watch your step. I recommend standing still when you first enter and waiting for your eyes to adjust to the darkness.'

'All good adventures start in the dark,' Shūichi commented, rubbing Kenta's hair.

The young man was looking into Shūichi's eyes, occasionally glancing at the half-hidden child behind him.

'Some people prefer to sit on the floor. Others report feeling a sense of claustrophobia due to the confined space. If that's the case, don't hesitate to come out and go back in when you feel ready.'

At that moment, three girls walked out of the Heart Room, whispering comments that none of them caught. Two seemed excited, while the other remained suspended.

'Here to the right, we have the "Listening Room",' the young man continued. 'That's a space where visitors can listen to all the recorded heartbeats in the archive through headphones. There are no rules for listening. You can search for someone with your surname or listen to the heartbeat of someone who lives in a city you have visited.'

Shūichi watched as the girls stood in front of the three stations. In front of them, behind the computers, headphones and keyboard, was a wide windowpane through which stripes of pale blue, azure blue and creamy white stretched: the sky, the sea and the sand.

'Finally, here on the left we have the "Recording Room".' The young man turned around completely, and only then did Shūichi notice two white doors blending into the wall. 'In there, using a special device, you can record the sound of your own heart. It will become part of the Heartbeat Archive.'

The quote written at the entrance to the Heartbeat Archive, which nobody noticed, not Shūichi, nor Kenta, nor any of that day's visitors

'My whole life I have not stopped accumulating evidence to stop things from disappearing, and, in the end, I have done nothing but reinforce their disappearance, accentuate the vision of this loss.'

—CHRISTIAN BOLTANSKI

Heart Room
ハートルーム

SHŪICHI GATHERED ALL THE THINGS that were dearest to him and lowered the handle. In the total darkness of the room, a light bulb hung from a cord. The bulb flashed on and off with the rhythm of the heartbeat that had just started.

Shūichi summoned his greatest loves, even the most recent, like Sayaka and Kenta, and the house where he had spent his childhood. With each flash, people came back into his mind, and places where he had stored memories, even sad ones, and books he had written over the years, each of which had

327

left a story etched in his soul. Like the one about the little protagonist who was shipwrecked; he visualised him as his skinny arms pushed aside vegetation and he ventured deeper into the island. The little boy with the features of Shingo who appeared to Shūichi every time he picked up a pencil – because every child, before being a child, was Shingo. Then, after a moment, his son would rise, wander off, and the other child, the protagonist of the story, would begin to live his own life.

Shūichi took a step forward, then another. Kenta took hold of his hand, and he squeezed it.

Then the sound of the heartbeat ceased, and the room fell into total darkness.

Six long seconds of darkness and silence, and the recording of another heartbeat began, faster, perhaps belonging to a young person or someone who had been running.

Kenta let go of his hand.

Shūichi focused his thoughts on Sayaka. She had told him one night that she loved things with an unstable light: a light bulb nearing its end, the point where something that couldn't be broken, broke.

Shūichi recalled the sun in his childhood, marking

328

the time on the walls of his house. Back then, he never stopped to think about it because it was all normal, but after moving to Tōkyō, he began to appreciate how wonderful it was to grow up in a house different from all the others, with a garden like the wall around a well, protecting its inhabitants from the outside world, which he would wander around, together with the light.

As Shūichi observed the filaments of the bulb lighting up and extinguishing to the rhythm of someone's heartbeat, he remembered Shingo's heart. He had heard it for the first time in the hospital, inside Aya's faintly visible belly, and later at home, using a device with headphones they had purchased online. It was supposed to check the well-being of the foetus even when it wasn't moving. Shūichi remembered the night he woke up abruptly and saw his wife's shadow next to him. Aya was hunched over, the headphones pressed to her ears, and her voice cracking with anguish: 'I can't hear him, I can't hear him!' In the end, they got rid of the device because it increased her anxiety rather than alleviating it.

Right then, Kenta took his hand and Shūichi

returned to the Heart Room. He realised the boy was finding the room scary.

'Do you want to go outside?' he whispered.

'What are they? On the walls?'

'Black mirrors, Chilean. They show your soul rather than your face.'

'I'm scared.'

'Let's go outside.'

Listening Room
リスニングルーム

THE THREE STATIONS IN THE Listening Room were still occupied by the girls, so Kenta and Shūichi sat on the bench.

The young man in the white shirt was explaining to an elderly couple what this place was. They had stumbled upon it by chance. 'We thought we were heading to the Heart Archive Centre in Teshima.'

The Heart Archive Centre was a small space run by the local community to preserve the memory of the island's ecological recovery; the legal battle the inhabitants of Teshima, Naoshima, and other islands in the archipelago had fought against the government in the 1970s. They accused the government of illegally disposing of industrial waste on their islands. That place also had the word 'heart' in its name, and the young man in the white shirt smiled.

'Your confusion is perfectly normal,' he reassured them. He said that at least two or three people every week ended up there by mistake.

'Are you OK?' Shūichi asked Kenta, who seemed to have calmed down. 'Feeling better?'

The boy nodded.

'I want to go back inside the dark room. But later.'

'Later? When?'

'When I'm older.'

Shūichi squeezed his shoulder. 'OK, we'll do that.'

When two of the three girls left their stations, Shūichi and Kenta got up and went into the Listening Room.

The young man in the white shirt accompanied the elderly couple to the exit, then walked over to where Kenta was sitting and started to explain how to choose a heart on the database, and how to read the people's information.

'If they recorded their heartbeat here in Teshima,

the visitors have the opportunity to leave a message, but not all of them do.'

'OK, thank you,' Kenta said. He seemed anxious to put on the headphones.

'Take your time and concentrate on listening,' the man said as he walked away.

Shūichi jumped at random from one name to another, from Greece to Italy, from Poland to Tasmania. He listened to the hearts of Neil Charm Calub, who had written that he came to the Heartbeat Archive 'With Celine Joly, for whom this heart beats', and Wakaba Tanaka who had recorded his twenty-four-year-old heart. He intended to search for Anna Bernini, who had left her beat at the Hangar Bicocca in Milan in September eleven years earlier. Who knows what has happened to her in the past eleven years, he thought, whether when she recorded it she was young or old, whether she's still alive, what she does, who she is.

Every so often, Shūichi glanced over the divider that separated him from Kenta. But the boy looked absorbed in listening.

A German heart, a Swiss heart, a Chinese heart, a Korean heart, Shūichi thought looking at him, we work hard to try to be different our whole lives, but we end up identical to the original plan.

These were testimonies that all of these people had been alive; that a part of them was infinitely replicable.

He put the headphones back on and chose another number at random.

The last one was the heart of Arima Hanane. A few seconds after it started, the heartbeat mixed with the loud sound of crying. It had been recorded just a few days earlier, in the same place where he was now sitting, his eyes filled with mustard-coloured sand and the Inland Sea of Japan stretching out in front of him. Shūichi saw that there was an accompanying message and clicked on it: 'I am zero years old, and I came with mummy and daddy.'

Kenta was the first to stand up, and Shūichi followed shortly after. They returned to sit on the bench by the entrance.

The owners of the four hearts Kenta and Shūichi heard in the Listening Room

Guillame Cluzet	38 years old	Centre Pompidou, Paris, 2013/02/03
Mario de Santis	53 years old	Museo Mambo, Bologna, 2016/06/26
Christian Boltanski	65 years old	Serpentine Gallery, London, 2010/07/06
Mara Tsafantaki	–	Onassis Cultural Centre, Athens, 2012/12/28

Recording Room
レコーディングルーム

IN THE BREAK BETWEEN ONE room and the next, Shūichi and Kenta leafed through the books and the catalogue that were on sale.

Shūichi asked the young woman behind the reception – who in the meantime had taken over from the young man – if she was originally from Teshima and why she too was wearing a white shirt. She responded that yes, both she and the man before were from Teshima, and that this was how the artist had wanted the space: white walls, medical-style shirts, to reproduce the aesthetic environment of a visit to the cardiologist.

The doors to the Recording Rooms opened and the girls who had preceded them in all the stages walked out.

'Would you prefer to go in together?' Shūichi asked, but Kenta shook his head.

They each went into a separate room and closed the door behind them.

Shūichi would never forget what happened in the Recording Room.

Shūichi opened his shirt, ran his fingers, as he always did, along the scar from the operation, and picked up the recording instrument that had, like the stethoscope, a plate attached to its end. He sat down on the black leather chair, calmed his breath and pressed the drum to the skin over his heart.

He sat in complete silence, careful not to rustle the fabric of his shirt.

There it was, the familiar sound of his own heart. It suddenly seemed curious that he had listened to it so many times that it was lodged in his memory, and yet he had never had the desire to record it.

338

He relistened with the headphones that hung next to the screen. It was possible to record it again, if you weren't satisfied with how it had come out. He thought, all things considered, it had gone pretty well, and was nervous that Kenta, in the next room, might need help or have already finished.

It was only when Shūichi pressed the confirmation button and his name, surname, age and place appeared on the screen, and he realised he didn't have a message to leave but that it was sufficient, at the end of the day, just to help grow that special archive, that he saw the code.

A code was created automatically for each recording: a sequence of numbers that would accompany his heartbeat forever.

The code, five figures, started with 4 and ended with 9.

He closed everything in a hurry: the file on the computer, his shirt buttons. His mind not there, he put everything back and found himself outside, on the right of the counter with the young woman in the white shirt on the computer, and Kenta who had not yet come out of his own little room.

Shūichi sat down on the bench and started to

rummage around in his rucksack. His fingers were shaking and his heart had risen up into his mouth. He breathed, feeling all the force of his lungs, his blood pumping, full of fear that it was just a coincidence.

Could it be? he kept asking himself. Could it be possible?

He pulled out of the inside pocket of his wallet the photo of Shingo, the one of Aya and him in their twenties, a black and white one of his mother. He moved the little beating-heart-shaped *origami* that Aya had given him and that had remained there, next to the most precious memories of his life. At the bottom, still rolled up, were the two pieces of paper that he had found months ago in the little box in his mother's drawer, with the Post-it attached: 'For Shūichi'.

He remembered sensing their mystery, their secrecy, right from the start, and how he had racked his brain for weeks without finding a solution. He had even sought help from Kenta, but to no avail. Periodically, those numbers resurfaced, begging to be deciphered. But Shūichi pushed them away, incapable of giving them meaning.

42191.

42192.

Could it be? Could they have something to do with that place?

When Kenta came out of the room, he didn't notice Shūichi's distorted face.

'Done!' he exclaimed cheerfully. He'd had fun recording his own heartbeat and listening back to it.

Shūichi stood up abruptly. 'Excuse me,' he asked the young woman, 'would it be possible to go back into the Listening Room?'

'Of course, there's no time limit. You can go back to the Heart Room or the Listening Room. Recording, however, is only possible once. Take your time.'

'Thank you.' Then, turning to the boy: 'Kenta, do you mind if I search for something in the archive? Maybe in the meantime, you can call your mum and dad or send them a message.'

'OK,' Kenta replied, only then noticing the strained expression on Shūichi's face.

Shūichi handed him his phone and went to sit down at the database in the Listening Room.

From a distance, Kenta observed his hunched back. He sensed the turmoil in his movements but

341

remained silent.

Meanwhile, through the rectangle of the window, the sea had grown darker. The sun was descending, and in an hour, the evening would set the beach alight with orange, followed shortly by a darkness that would devour everything.

One by one

4

2

1

9

1

Click. A grey page opened. He was consumed by emotion. It wasn't a coincidence! It wasn't a coincidence!

Shūichi read:

'*Ōno Reina*, 76 years old.'

Shūichi's heart was racing. He placed his palm on his chest like his mother always told him. Stop, breathe.

How was it possible that his mother had been there and he knew nothing about it? He searched the profile again for an answer and found it in the date.

The recording was from two and a half years ago; the day coincided with the week Shūichi had spent in the hospital having his surgery. There was no accompanying message, and later Shūichi thought it wasn't necessary. It wouldn't add anything to the wonder he was feeling now.

He immediately understood who the other code belonged to.

4

2

1

9

2

He knew what was written on the screen before looking up at it:

'*Maeda Shingo*, 8 years old.'

The sound of Mrs Ōno's heart and the sound of Shingo's heart

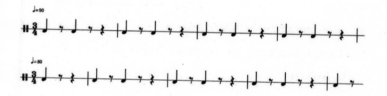

Kenta and Shūichi were the last visitors to leave the Heartbeat Archive in Teshima that day.

While the boy was outside examining the sand, Shūichi went to the counter, trembling, and asked the young woman if it was possible to obtain the recordings of his son's and mother's heartbeats. His voice seemed to come from afar, as if he were living two lives, one real, the other inside him.

A few phone calls and an email address were exchanged, and there was a promise of contact within seventy-two hours.

As Shūichi left the building, he observed Kenta playing. He was touched by his small shadow elongated by the sun and tugged along by his running. He thought about how the word 'heart' was rooted in language, in every language on the planet, to the point that it had always seemed to him like an organism with a thousand ties, a little jungle creature that, instead of swinging from vines, twirled and clung to veins and arteries.

But now it seemed like a new word to him, one that was capable of multiplying.

'Kenta!' he called from a distance.

The child arrived with a stick in hand, his face flushed.

'I'm done, sorry for making you wait.'

'What's that?' Kenta asked, pointing his little stick in the air.

Shūichi looked up and saw a dark mass. It was stuck on one of the trees in the forest they had crossed to reach the Archive. It was surrounded by branches and twigs that stood out against an increasingly dark blue backdrop.

'A bird's nest.'

It looked like a heart, its upper arteries injecting life into the world.

The air, the sky, were infused with blood.

'The last boat to Takamatsu leaves from the port of Teshima in fifty minutes, we need to hurry.'

Shūichi started saying that he had found something

in the Archive, but he stopped himself. Instead he said that the weather had turned cloudy, that it might rain the following day.

Kenta didn't say anything but continued to observe his friend, in that delicate way that just about touched him.

There was much they could have said, but they preferred to stay silent. Shūichi because the emotion was too much; Kenta because, without understanding, he intuited something. It was a fitting preparation for the return journey.

They waited ten minutes for the bus and another fifteen for the boat. They saw the lights come on over the sea, and as they drifted further away, the lamp posts began to flicker on too.

When darkness swallowed the horizon, they were at sea, far from all the islands of the archipelago.

They returned to the *ryokan* where they had left their luggage in the morning. Dinner was ready.

The waitresses, wearing *kimono*, entered the room carrying large trays and explained the dishes in detail. They unravelled them one by one like knots and presented the story of each ingredient: where the crabs had been caught, what else the shellfish shells were used for on the islands, that the flour for the *udon* noodles was produced in the area, by far the best flour in the country.

Kenta was ravenous; Shūichi ate slowly.

In the intervals between one dish and the next, Shūichi tapped his fingers on the table. Kenta looked at him with curiosity. It seemed like the rhythm of something he was trying to hold onto.

What the critic Yoshitani Matsuo wrote about Shūichi's book in that year's October edition of Moe magazine

Since the beginning of his artistic career, Maeda Shūichi has shrouded the faces of the child protagonists of his books in mist. In this book, little S-kun is shipwrecked on an (almost) deserted island, while in the previous work, *The Tree of Memory*, Akira-kun dives into the swimming pool of an apartment building in a bustling city and establishes his own life in its depths. What unites them all, from book to book, is a certain vagueness of their features. Upon closer examination, Maeda renders the young protagonists unrecognisable yet precise, because they are exactly the child we have before us, the one that eludes us, the one who may disappear tomorrow to make way for the adult they are destined to become: they are all ghosts of a childhood about to end.

Compared to Maeda Shūichi's previous works,

The Shipwreck introduces a rupture. If, until now, the artist has accustomed us to real or imaginary journeys carried out solo from beginning to end, with soft colours that easily transition into shades of grey, here, in his last very colourful (and very successful!) illustration, the boy protagonist – who seemed destined to explore the island without encountering others of his kind – encounters his own image reflected in the surface of a lake, extends his hand, and pulls another child, very similar to himself, out of the water, to begin a new adventure. Maeda is suggesting, perhaps, that two solitudes can become a companionship. That the world, when seen through two pairs of eyes, can take on colour.

Epilogue

TESHIMA, FOR YEARS ENVELOPED IN heartbeats and polished by the waves, begins to pulse at ten in the morning and finishes its song at four or five at night. It depends on the season, the time when the sun goes down.

'The Island of Heartbeats' is what Kenta would call it when telling his parents about the adventure. And since then, for all of them, it would always be known as that.

Shūichi and Kenta bid farewell to Teshima without too much nostalgia, certain they would be back.

As soon as he landed in Tōkyō, Shūichi sent a message to Sayaka inviting her to dinner. They had long abandoned restaurant outings and chance encounters. There was no need to pretend any more, to try to appear something more than they were. That was the beauty of a love that began big; accepting each other's misery and absurdity was, in fact, the truest test of love.

In front of a takeaway meal drowning in sauces, Shūichi retraced his journey with Kenta, the Teshima Archive, his mother and Shingo's heartbeats that he had learned by heart.

Sayaka was moved to tears when he reproduced the distinct sound of the two hearts with his fingertips and voice, just as he had obstinately repeated throughout the return journey, so as not to forget them. They had become like a song you can't get out of your head.

In Teshima, Shūichi said, there was evidence that his mother and son had been alive, that a replicable part of them (as well as the thousands of other people who had shared that experience) existed forever. That's when he realised that memory was a matter of will, nothing else.

'When did they go to the island?'

Shūichi reconstructed for Sayaka the journey of his mother and son: it had happened exactly two and a half years earlier, when he was having his surgery.

'The scar on your chest?'

'Yes, that's the one.'

He had had to stay in the hospital, and Shūichi had asked his mother to take Shingo on a short trip, preferably to the sea, so that he wouldn't go through the stress of the operation and Aya's anxiety. He thought that only a bigger memory would be capable of pushing aside that other memory, or at least make it a little less significant.

Sayaka couldn't help smiling because Shūichi was just like Mrs Ōno in his attempts to minimise and push away the pain, to make it small in his son's memory. She didn't tell him, but she laid a hand on his cheek as he continued talking.

Aya was terrified of her husband's surgery, fearing that Shūichi might die. That's why they all agreed that taking Shingo away from Tōkyō to do something fun would be the best solution.

They had started months before, setting every-thing up, subjecting him to the long, often senseless conversations that adults hope in vain will prepare children.

On the day of departure, Shingo's suitcase was small. Inside it was a white teddy bear, three swimsuits, a sketchbook, pencils, and a new electronic encyclopaedia his father had given him. The destination was chosen for its convenience so that grandmother and grandson wouldn't have to exert themselves: a comfortable seaside hotel on the nearby peninsula of Miura.

But Shūichi knew now that they hadn't been in Miura, at least not for the entire holiday.

He would never know the circumstances in which his mother had found out about Teshima. One day, he would find the article clipping that had sparked the idea, but he wouldn't be able to reconstruct the wonderful coincidence that two weeks before Shūichi's heart surgery, his mother had read about the island in a magazine at the hair salon. The artist's words about collecting people's heartbeats as a tribute to life were like an epiphany to her.

'It's the perfect place for our trip, don't you think?' she had said to her grandson on the morning of their departure.

The child was unaware that they were heading to the airport. He thought they were going to take only one train, get off at the end of the line, and then three stops on the bus. Mrs Ōno had decided not to tell the child anything, partly because she wanted it to be a genuine surprise, and partly because she feared Shūichi and Aya would try to change her mind.

'But, Grandma, isn't it too far?'

'Maybe, but it's an adventure. Don't you like adventures?'

'Yes, but . . .'

'Then let's go! We'll be back the day after tomorrow and then off to the Miura hotel as originally planned, I promise!'

Shūichi's mother thought that visiting the Archive would be a good-luck charm, a gift to her son as well as to herself. Shingo, who trusted his grandmother, didn't object any further and set off with Loretto the bear in his suitcase, the stuffed animal handed down to him by his father years ago.

Shūichi wondered why his mother had never mentioned the trip to him. It was probably for the same reason she had hidden the photographs of

Shingo in her room: his mother gave up opportunities for joy in order to avoid awakening pain.

That evening, Sayaka listened to the story of the discovery, asking about every detail of the trip to Teshima, about Kenta, about the excursions they had made to Naoshima and Konpira-gu, the rocking boat, and the plane ride from Takamatsu.

Then, as if emptied of words, Sayaka and Shūichi went to bed without saying anything more to each other.

The next morning, they woke at dawn. The sky opened up, light streamed down in waves, and the sea changed colour. They caught a glimpse of it as they walked down towards the café where they were heading for breakfast.

The day was there, brand new.

While eating a slice of carrot cake, Shūichi watched as Sayaka spilled her latte and believed he could see her multiple faces all at once. How many expressions had he seen on her face during those months? She who threw open seasons and windows with the same amazement, as if she believed she would always find something more beyond them.

'Can I ask you a question?' Sayaka suddenly said. 'I've read all your books, and the windows . . .'

Windows, years on, remained Shūichi's great obsession.

'Why do you draw windows?' dozens, hundreds of times he had been asked. 'Perhaps because you're interested in knowing what's outside?' Yet, the windows Shūichi drew were all drawn from the outside looking in, from the street, from a bridge, from a station, or a park, standing beside or in front of them.

Shūichi had only answered that question once, during a book launch. That's why he didn't like doing public talks; he didn't like the questions. But that afternoon, a five-year-old boy had raised his hand, and Shūichi looked him straight in the eyes and saw that among all those adults who were full of answers, only he truly wanted to know.

'Why do you draw windows? And why do you always draw them from the outside?'

'I'm interested in knowing what's inside more than what's outside,' he had said. 'From the street, if you think about it, you can only see a tiny part of the inside of a house. But for the person looking,

359

maybe a piece of the ceiling, a chandelier, a drawing on the wall, that tiny part becomes the whole house.'

Shūichi had paused, and observed the people in the bookshop who were listening attentively.

'Do you ever look at the lit windows in the evening when you're coming home from school?'

The child had nodded.

'Well, you see, I like the idea that what makes a house happy or sad, and what makes the family or the child living in it happy or sad, can only be understood from the outside, looking in, when you're walking home from the station after school, imagining, maybe while holding your mother's hand.'

From that point in the conversation, the day crumbled in his memory, but Shūichi remembered looking at the child again, widening his pupils to embrace all of his concentration, his serious face, and the multiple illuminated and darkened windows towards which, from that afternoon onward, he would look.

Shūichi lowered the fork he was bringing to his mouth and asked Sayaka, 'Do you want to know why I always draw windows?'

But she shook her head.

'No, but on the way home, I'd like to take you to see the windows of the house I grew up in.'

'That would be nice.'

'I would like you to remember them.'

Carrying his surfboard down to the beach at dawn, Shūichi saw the sea and nothing on the horizon. Not a cloud, nor a surfer. From that perspective, the earth looked deserted. It felt like the first day on the planet.

That morning, he would teach Sayaka and Kenta how to surf and, worried about not being there when they arrived, he had gone down before the sun came up. They had arranged to meet at six.

Shūichi sat on the beach, waiting. He felt happy, but his happiness was marbled by the knowledge that even the things he loved the most would come to an end.

Once again, after years, he loved and was loved. There was even a child in his life.

The thought that he could start over – a meaningful relationship, the fear of being alone, the shoelaces to watch, misunderstandings, grazes on elbows and knees – was dizzying.

Now the world couldn't collapse again, couldn't fall apart so easily. It needed to hold up for the time of that child and the things that child loves. Another hundred years at least? Perhaps two hundred?

Everything, for Shūichi, gained meaning, and at the same time, fear clung to him: cars driving too fast, bicycle lights that needed checking so he wouldn't ride in the dark like some kids carelessly did, tall and sharp rocks he could fall from, global warming and plastic in the ocean. He felt a pull to join the people he saw on the beach in the early mornings and evenings with bags and pincers in hand, picking litter.

At that moment, a noisy group of boys ran past, plunging into the water with their surfboards. The sunrise was now all around.

Shūichi sighed. It took such energy to be happy when you weren't yet.

But his mother was right: to be happy, first of all you need to imagine being happy.

While he was still immersed in those thoughts, Sayaka and Kenta arrived behind him.

'Here we are!' Sayaka exclaimed cheerfully. 'We bumped into each other on the way, riding our bikes.'

She held a white and geranium-red board under her arm, with stripes along the edges. She had borrowed it from a friend. The boy appeared to be holding his board by a leash, a rope tugging behind it a small cobalt blue plank.

'It's beautiful here!'

'Are you both ready?'

Shūichi looked at the water and the boy. He was about to ask him if he felt safe, to check he wasn't afraid of diving into that boundless thing of which humans actually know so little.

But he said nothing.

'And so, how do you surf?' Kenta asked, captivated by the sight of the rippling sea. 'I can't wait to ride a wave!'

'We're very excited,' Sayaka whispered.

Shūichi picked up his own board and stood next to them. Sayaka on his right, Kenta on his left. The three of them facing out towards the sea.

He was unaware that his heart was making a lot of noise.

'So,' Shūichi said, 'first of all, look at the sea.'

'And then?' asked Kenta, impatient.

'And then, imagine yourself standing on your board, out there in the middle of the waves.'

The sounds of the heart in Japanese

baku baku ばくばく the sound of a heart that's nervous or tense; represents a heartbeat that is getting faster in frequency, almost painful.

doki doki どきどき the sound of an excited heart, the cardiac acceleration that occurs when you are afraid of something that is about to happen; it is also the result of a joyful wait, a future event that's getting closer or a desire about to be realised.

It's the sound of a heart that's growing and learning life; the moment that precedes the emotion and therefore, more than its realisation, it's the emotion itself.

dokin ドキン a single beat, occurring only once, for example on love at first sight when the heart seems to skip a beat.

dokitto ドキッと a beat agitated by a narrowly escaped danger, like a lie that was almost uncovered or a falling object miraculously saved.

dokkun dokkun ドックンドックン a strong, highly agitated beat; the excitement, for example, that precedes stepping onto a stage for a performance, or meeting a loved one.

toku toku とくとく a small beat with a quiet voice; the sound, for example, of the heart of a newborn baby.

An important note

EW PEOPLE KNOW BUT I am the daughter of a
manuscript plucked from the pile.

Over time, retracing my steps in my memory, I
have come to believe that while talent may be necessary (who knows if I had any), the quality that leads
to success, regardless of the context, is perseverance.
It is not believing too much in a predetermined
fate, pushing the boundaries of how you imagine
yourself, one step at time and − just observing −
doing other things.

If at eighteen I hadn't believed in what didn't yet

exist, if in the despair of twenty-one I hadn't nurtured my imagination of the me that didn't exist, I'm certain I would never have printed a manuscript in a small university copy shop on the outskirts of Tōkyō, I wouldn't have sent that stack of pages to fifteen Italian publishing houses. I wouldn't have waited.

Above all, I wouldn't have continued writing throughout the years when I received no response – learning, however, the greatest lesson: that not succeeding is never an excuse. It's necessary to try other paths because there are a thousand ways home. Serenity, I've told myself since then, should be like coming home after imagining oneself on a journey, even standing still, wheels on the ground, spending the night on a park bench, the moon obscured.

Imagining myself happy is still my biggest challenge. Something that I believe will require daily practice until the end. However, sending that manuscript – having the courage to do so – reminds me that everything starts with the annunciation of a loud 'yes' to life. Trying, in the meantime, and imagining that it will succeed. The rest will follow.

Happiness, as Leo Tolstoy understood it, is always the right answer, the one thing you can bet on and never go wrong. In his diaries, he wrote: 'He who is happy is right.'

The summer of 2021 marked the end of a two-year period painted in dark shades, coinciding largely with the pandemic and an emotional restlessness that left me in episodes, conversations and company that I could have done without. I distinctly remember at least three times when, curled up on the bed, in tears, I begged Ryōsuke to take care of the children, to take them out somewhere, because simply breathing, being alive, being there, weighed so heavily on me. I seriously feared I was falling into a depression. However, since the end of that frozen summer, I haven't felt that way again. It was then, after the Tōkyō Olympics, that I set out to visit Teshima, Naoshima, and many other islands in the Seto Inland Sea of Japan.

Visiting the Heartbeat Archive, *Les Archives du Coeur*, or, as it is translated in Japanese (and from which my chosen wording originates), *Shinzō-on no Ākaibu*, made me feel life again. I immediately knew I was going to write about it.

Everything came rushing back to me: the long years of my doctorate at the Tōkyō University of Foreign Studies, Professor Hideo Matsuura speaking to me about Christian Boltanski, my teenage ear pressed against the chest of my boyfriend, memorising the sound I wanted to carry with me, the restless heartbeat of Sōsuke in the Tōkyō clinic (assuring me that he was alive, despite having been told otherwise weeks earlier), the autobiographical-biographical dialogue, *The Possible Life of Christian Boltanski*, and three ideas that were revolutionary for me.

The first was that lies invent life, even make it better, and that everything we remember has more to do with the narrative of the life we live (which is always imprecise, inevitably personal, never object-ive) rather than the truth (which doesn't exist, it doesn't!). The second was that there is nothing we can do: if we renounce pain, joy disappears with it! The third taught me that the most robust form of happiness is in the third person; with first-person happiness, we have too much power, we can create and undo it as we please. In my diary, in the August of that summer, I wrote: 'And so my joy shifts into third person. Sōsuke didn't go to nursery this morning. I wanted him with us. To make the experience beautiful, I distracted myself from myself, which is always the greatest gift I can give myself. I also adored June because I was so immersed in a teenage feeling, a girl's feeling, that I forgot about my own life, and I truly rested. But now there is a different quality of happiness, even more intense, perhaps the only one that can be planned, the one directed not towards ourselves but towards others. Yes, I am ready for third-person happiness!'

A few months later, this novel was born.

While writing *The Library of Heartbeats*, I remembered the precious exhortation of a friend during those darkest days: 'Even if you feel bad, even if you don't want to, go out with the children, pretend to be happy, pretend to have fun with them, but you must believe it, believe it seriously, otherwise it doesn't count.' That's the imagination of happiness: to be happy, first of all you need to imagine being happy!

That August of 2021, at the Heartbeat Archive on Teshima, I recorded the sound of my heart, and left a message for my children. I boarded the boat, leaving the island behind, already enveloped in darkness, with the conviction that from certain places, you never leave, that a part of them is deposited inside us. The Heartbeat Archive, just like the Wind Phone had been years before, was one of those places.

In an instant, I saw Sasaki-san again, the guardian of the Wind Phone in Bell Gardia. Sitting at the table on his veranda, in a calm and firm voice, he told me that the most important thing was to cultivate children's imagination because the Wind Phone doesn't work without imagination. That's why it is necessary to surround children with books and nature.

Over these years, I have come to understand that without imagination, nothing works.

Glossary

adzuki: variety of small, reddish-brown beans, a fundamental ingredient in Japanese baking, from which *an* (red bean paste) is made.

dorayaki: a type of Japanese sweet consisting of two pancakes sandwiched together with a red bean paste filling in the centre. There are numerous variations on the filling.

kanji: ideographic characters of Chinese origin that, along with *hiragana* and *katakana*, constitute the writing system of the Japanese language.

konbini: convenience stores open twenty-four hours a day, seven days a week, 365 days a year.

kotatsu: a low table with a wooden frame that has a source of heat underneath, traditionally used in Japanese homes during the colder seasons of the year.

mangaka: a comic-book (manga) artist.

onigiri: boiled rice pressed into spherical or triangular shapes, filled with pickled plums, salmon pieces, or other ingredients, often wrapped in seaweed.

origami: Japanese art of folding paper.

ryokan: traditional Japanese inn.

tako-tsubo: 'tako-tsubo syndrome' or 'broken heart syndrome' is a mostly transient cardiomyopathy caused by acute stress of physical or psychological origin, which results in the dysfunction of the left ventricle. Its name (literally 'octopus vase') comes from the term used in Japanese to refer to a trap

for octopuses, whose shape resembles that of a
heart affected by this condition.

Tanabata: a celebration that falls on 7 July or 7 August
every year.

tanuki: creatures from Japanese mythology, similar to
raccoon dogs, that enjoy shape-shifting, playing
pranks and deceiving people.

tanzaku: a strip of paper used to write haiku or tanka
verses or wishes on, to hang on bamboo branches
during the *Tanabata* celebration in July/August.

tomo-biki: derived from *tomo*, meaning 'friends', and
hiki, *hiku*, which means 'to pull', so it means 'to
pull friends towards oneself'. According to super-
stition, holding a funeral on a *tomo-biki* day would
mean bringing friends and acquaintances to the
grave, hence the day of rest.

udon: a variety of soft wheat noodles, usually served
in broth.

umeboshi: salted plum with health-giving properties.

yuzu: a particular variety of Japanese citrus fruit, similar to a bergamot.

zō-mushi: or curculionoidea are insects of the order Coleoptera. The Japanese name *zō-mushi* (literally 'elephant bug') is due to the elongation of the head, resembling an elephant's trunk, an organ with which they puncture and deposit eggs in the tissue of plants.

References

The quote on page 120 is from Emil Cioran, *The Fall into Time*, Quadrangle Books, 1970, translated by Richard Howard; on page 177 from Elias Canetti, *The Secret Heart of the Clock*, Farrar, Straus and Giroux, 1989, translated by Joel Agee; on page 250 from Maurice Pinguet, *La Mort volontaire au Japon* (Voluntary Death in Japan), Gallimard, 1984, translated by Lucy Rand; on pages 267–8 from Sei Shōnagon, *The Pillow Book*, Oxford University Press, 1967, translated by Ivan Morris; on page 287 from Walt Whitman, 'Song of Myself', *Leaves of Grass*, David MacKay, 1892; on page 315 from Friedrich Dürrenmatt, *Das Sterben der Pythia* (The Death of the Pythia), Diogenes Verlag, 1971, translated by Lucy Rand.

Boltanski, Christian, Catherine Grenier, *La vie possible de Christian Boltanski* [The Possible Life of Christian Boltanski], Seuil, Paris, 2007.

Fukutake Foundation (edited by), *Christian Boltanski. Les archives du coeur*, Nissa Printing, Naoshima, 2012.

Kurashima, Atsushi, Minoru Harada, *Ame no kotoba jiten* [Dictionary of Words for Rain], Kōdansha, Tōkyō, 2014.

Miyakoshi, Akiko, *Yoru no kaerimichi* [The Way Home in the Night], Kaiseisha, Tōkyō, 2015.

von Borstel, Johannes Hinrich, *Heart*, Scribe, London, 2016 (English translation by David Shaw).

Thanks

THE HAND THAT GRABBED THAT first manuscript belongs to the first person who believed in me and has continued to do so without hesitation over the years: Francesca Lang. For this reason, *The Library of Heartbeats* is dedicated to her, thus repaying a little, at least in words, the debt contracted almost ten years ago. I will be forever grateful to her for that gesture.

Thanks to my first readers, Cristina Banella and Mario De Santis. Thank you for holding my hand throughout the entire time. Thanks to Paola Cantatore for her beautiful friendship, and to Rita Scinardi, who has explained fundamental things to me over the years.

THE LIBRARY OF HEARTBEATS

Thanks to my agents, Monica Malatesta, Simone Marchi, Francesca Asciolla, and the entire team at MalaTesta Agency, who have given me the serenity and clarity to allow me to do my best work. And to the Piemme team, who immediately embraced this novel.

A special thanks to Mario Pireddu, a friend and musician who carefully studied the heartbeats and composed music for them: 'The sound of Mrs Ōno's heart and the sound of Shingo's heart' are his work.

Thanks to Chiara Tiveron, who granted me access to an out-of-print book, and to Valentina Carnelutti, who agreed to give this novel a voice, her beautiful voice.

Thanks to Sōsuke, my son, the artist behind the drawing of Loretto the bear. Thanks to Emilio's little heart that clings so often to mine. Thanks to Ryōsuke, the most important family I have.

To write novels, I almost always read essays, dozens of essays. I identify the topic and then go through it extensively: each time it feels like I'm writing a doctoral thesis and at the same time opening doors and windows in and outside of myself. Thanks, once again, to the dozens of books and authors who have explained to me – often reprimanding me – why the theme of the heart is so far from trivial. It is, as Christian Boltanski said, what makes us unique and, at the same time, close to one another: 'the heartbeat is the greatest symbol of human life . . . on the one hand, it explains how everyone is part of the same family, and on the other, it expresses the intrinsic fact that two people are not the same.'

Kamakura, Summer 2022

If you loved *The Library of Heartbeats,* then you might enjoy *The Phone Box at the Edge of the World*

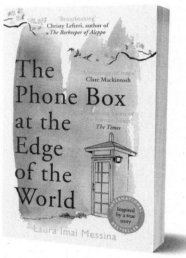

The Phone Box at the Edge of the World
is an unforgettable story of the depths of grief, the
lightness of love and the human longing to keep the people
who are no longer with us close to our hearts.

'Absolutely breathtaking' - Christy Lefteri, *Sunday Times*
bestselling author of *The Beekeeper of Aleppo.*

Read on for an extract

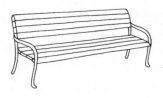

Prologue

IN THE VAST, STEEP GARDEN of Bell Gardia, great gusts of wind lashed the plants.

The woman instinctively raised an elbow to her face, rounding her back. Then, almost immediately, she straightened up again.

She had arrived before dawn, and watched as the light came up but the sun remained hidden. She had unloaded the big sacks from the car: fifty metres of maximum-thickness plastic rolled up in a tube, cylinders of electrical tape, ten boxes of ring-shank nails to attach to the ground and a hammer with a ladies' handle. At Conan, the enormous hardware store, a shop assistant had asked if she would mind showing him her hands. He just wanted to measure her grip, he said, but she had found herself frozen, unable to respond.

She hurried towards the phone box now. It looked fragile, as if it were made of candy canes and crumbling meringue. The wind was raging already; she didn't have much time.

They worked non-stop on the hill above Ōtsuchi for two hours: she – wrapping the phone box, the bench, the entrance sign and the little archway at the beginning of the path in tarpaulin – and the wind, which didn't let up for a moment. Every so often she would hug herself involuntarily, the way she had done for years whenever she felt her emotions rising up. But then she would get back on her feet, lengthen her spine and face the bank of clouds that now enshrouded the entire hill.

Only once she had finished, once she could taste the sea in her mouth, as if the world had been turned on its head, did she stop. Exhausted, she sat down on the bench, which she'd wrapped up like a silk-worm in its cocoon, feeling the weight of her boots, their soles packed with earth.

If the world were to fall now, she told herself, she would fall with it, but if there was even the slightest chance of it staying upright, she would use every last ounce of energy she had to make that happen.

The city below was still asleep. There was the odd window lit by the glow of a lamp, but most people had left their roller shutters down and secured their rain screens with wooden rods, in preparation for the approaching typhoon. Some had leaned sandbags against doors to prevent them from being ripped off their hinges by the fury of the wind and to stop the rain from flooding the rooms inside.

Yet Yui seemed oblivious to the rain and the dense blackness of the sky. She observed her work: the plastic and tape dressings she had used to protect the phone box, the wooden bench, the pathway of slabs in single file, the archway, and the signpost that read 'THE WIND PHONE'.

Everything was caked in mud and thoroughly waterlogged. If the typhoon threatened any sort of damage, she would be there, ready to hold it all in place.

Yui was untouched by the most basic truth: that fragility does not reside in things so much as in flesh. An object can be repaired or replaced, but the body cannot. Perhaps it is stronger than the soul, which once broken can remain so forever, but it is weaker than wood, lead or iron. Her refusal to acknowledge this meant that she didn't, for a single moment, perceive the danger she was in.

'It's September already,' she sighed, contemplating the darkness of the sky that was approaching from the east. *Nagatsuki* 長月, 'the month of long nights', as it used to be called. Yet she had repeated that same phrase every month: it's October already, November, December. It's April already, she had said, and then it was May, and so on; in the never-ending list of days that began on 11th March 2011.

Every week had been a struggle; every month simply hours stacked up in the attic, for a future that might never arrive.